Mills
Best Seller Romance

A chance to read and collect some of the best-loved novels from Mills & Boon—the world's largest publisher of romantic fiction.

Every month, four titles by favourite Mills & Boon authors will be re-published in the *Best Seller Romance* series.

A list of other titles in the *Best Seller Romance* series can be found at the end of this book.

Anne Mather

COUNTRY OF
THE FALCON

MILLS & BOON LIMITED
LONDON · TORONTO

First published 1975
Australian copyright 1981
Philippine copyright 1981
This edition 1981

© Anne Mather 1975

ISBN 0 263 73625 3

Set in Linotype Plantin 10 on 11½ pt.

Made and printed in Great Britain by Richard Clay (The Chaucer Press) Ltd, Bungay, Suffolk

CHAPTER ONE

ALEXANDRA awoke with the familiar sensation of apprehension which came from knowing that any one of a dozen horrific creatures might have entered the hut during the night. She peered down warily from her hammock with the alertness which came from experience and saw to her relief that the mud-packed floor below appeared free from invaders. On her first morning there over a week ago, she had climbed down carelessly and almost trodden on an enormous spider which her host had calmly informed her was merely seeking refuge from the dampness of the tropical forest outside and was quite harmless so long as she didn't attempt to touch it or attack it. As Alexandra was totally incapable of doing anything but standing there with every hair on her head assuming a life of its own, either alternative was beyond her.

Now she slithered in a rather ungainly fashion to the floor and looked about her drearily, stretching her aching back. She was not used to sleeping in a hammock, but that was the least of her worries. This bare hut with its thatched roof and mud floor had been her home for the past eight days and would continue to be so, so long as the rivers remained in flood and her guide refused to take her upstream. And as each day passed, the conviction grew within her that her father would *not* be pleased to see her.

She sighed. It had seemed such a great adventure, sitting in the common room, discussing the idea of coming to Brazil with her friends, but her pitiful knowledge had not prepared her for the savage reality of the Amazon basin. Until then, it had been her father's place of work, and the more she was warned against doing anything impulsive, the more determined she became. All her life, she had rebelled against her father's resolution that she should acquire a good education while he went off to all the most exciting countries of the world and only saw his daughter for brief periods at holiday times. When she was younger, she had not minded so much. She had tried to understand that because her mother had died while accompanying her father on one of his expeditions to some outlandish place, he had naturally wanted to protect his only offspring from a similar fate. But as Alexandra grew older, she had begun to doubt the validity of this. Her mother had always been a rather delicate woman, following her husband more faithfully than enthusiastically, while Alexandra possessed her father's strength and determination. Or so she had thought...

She couldn't deny that most of the time she had been happy at school. She was a popular girl and as the school accommodated boys as well as girls, she had grown up accepting a certain amount of male admiration as her due. She was not conceited, but she was aware that she was attractive to the opposite sex. Tall and slim, with straight corn-coloured hair, she possessed the kind of lissom beauty much sought after by less fortunate females, and even the most casual of attire looked elegant on her.

- But she didn't feel very elegant now. The thin cotton shirt was creased and so, too, were the tight-fitting jeans which had become her usual sleeping attire. She had almost forgotten how delightful it was to shed one's clothes and climb between the sheets of a real bed, and how soft and relaxing an interior sprung mattress could be.

It was all her own fault, of course, but that didn't make it any easier to take. And how was she to know that she was to be delayed in this godforsaken spot indefinitely?

6

Her arrival in Los Hermanos had been a revelation. It had proved to be little more than a landing point along the river, with a collection of thatched-roofed huts, and a store and warehouse. Her guide, a wizened, monkey-faced little man provided by the tourist authority in Manaus, deposited her there with the storekeeper, and then, by the means of much gesticulation, went on to explain that there were rapids upstream and until the vastly swollen river subsided he would go no further. They had left the Rio Negro some fifty miles above Manaus, and had followed this tributary, the Velhijo, for almost a hundred miles. It had been a strange journey. At the junction between the mighty Negro and the narrower Velhijo, their puny craft had been forced upstream by the weight of the waters below, and to Alexandra, who had never seen a river run against the current before, it was a frightening phenomenon. Further upstream they encountered a stagnant pool, strewn with dead insects and littered with leaves, which her guide had endeavoured to explain was the point where the descending waters of the Velhijo balanced the pressure of the water being forced upstream. After that, the river ran normally again, but Alexandra couldn't help but shiver at the thought of negotiating that turbulent current on her way back.

Now she pushed aside the curtain of vine leaves which gave the hut a little privacy and emerged into the sunlight. The mornings were the best time of day. Apart from the fact that each day brought her a little nearer to seeing her father, she had the reassuring knowledge inside her that it would be several hours before she had to climb into that precarious hammock once more.

She looked round, aware of the speculative gazes of a group of Indian women sitting cross-legged around a campfire in the clearing. Naked children, some of them adorably sweet, played in the dirt, occasionally standing and staring at Alexandra with their thumbs stuck in their mouths. She had grown accustomed to being an object of curiosity, and as she was the only wholly white person in the settlement she was doubly so. The storekeeper, Santos, was of mixed Indian-Mexican origin, while her guide, Vasco, spoke Portuguese but looked more Indian than anything else.

Alexandra's own knowledge of foreign languages was limited to a fair grounding in French and German, and the merest smattering of Spanish, gleaned during holidays abroad. Santos, fortunately, spoke quite good English, but Vasco littered his speech with Portuguese words that quite often completely confused her. Still, she had managed to communicate with both of them and the rest of the time she had sweated and waited restlessly, growing daily more convinced that she should not have come. But if anyone had told her how remote Paradiablo was she would probably not have believed them...

The hut she had been given to occupy was set some way back from the river but within sight and sound of the store and warehouse on the landing. What food she ate was provided by Santos's cook, Maria, and now she walked slowly across the clearing towards the shaded verandah of the store. Here Santos had bamboo chairs and a table, and Alexandra had grown accustomed to sitting there for hours on end, flicking away the flies and watching the constant movement of the river.

Maria was putting out some of the starchy mandioca bread on the table which was the Indian's staple diet, and she looked up and smiled when Alexandra appeared. She was an Indian girl of indeterminate age, although Alexandra suspected she was no older than herself. Indian women aged more quickly and Alexandra had seen the way Santos treated her. She was pretty sure he kept the girl for other reasons than cooking, but Maria didn't seem to mind. There was a certain acceptance of her lot about her, and Alexandra wondered rather grimly how Women's Lib would make out here.

Santos appeared as Alexandra was drinking her second cup of coffee. Of all things the coffee here was excellent, and she felt quite sure that without it she would have found it difficult to remain resolute.

Santos was not very tall, but he was immensely fat, and Alexandra could never completely quell the surge of disgust she felt at the idea of he and Maria together. He had a long moustache, and thinning black hair which he combed across his bald pate. He was invariably smoking a cigar, and this morning was no exception.

'Ah, good morning, Mees Tempest!' he greeted her blandly, scratching the hairs on his chest visible between the open buttons of his shirt. 'Is a lovely morning, yes?'

'Lovely,' agreed Alexandra without enthusiam.

'The river—she is subsiding, yes? Yes,' he nodded.

Alexandra's head jerked up. 'You think so?'

He shrugged in typically Mexican fashion. 'I think.' He chuckled. 'We will get that lazy—good-for-nothing moving, yes?'

'Oh, I hope so.' Alexandra was fervent. She put down her coffee cup. 'How long will it take us to get to Paradiablo?'

'You ask this many times, Mees Tempest. I cannot say.' He shrugged again. 'Two days——' He spread his hands. 'Three days.'

'So long?' Alexandra tried not to feel perturbed. Two nights alone with Vasco were not absolutely acceptable to her. It wasn't that she was prudish; in other circumstances the idea of feeling any alarm at the prospect would not have occurred to her. But here—with nowhere to escape to except the jungle—that was something else. And there were still the rapids ...

Santos was studying her expressive face and now he said: 'You are worried about Vasco?' He shook his head.

11

'You will not be alone.'

'What do you mean?'

'I will send two Indian bearers with you.'

'Bearers?' Alexandra frowned. 'I don't understand.'

Santos lowered his bulk on to one of the cane chairs and Alexandra watched the narrow legs buckle a little. It always amazed her that they didn't snap altogether beneath his weight.

'The rapids, Mees Tempest.' He raised his eyebrows and at her look of incomprehension, he went on: 'Not all rapids are—how do you say it?—*negociavel*?'

'Negotiable?' offered Alexandra, and he nodded.

'*Sim*, negotiable.' He stretched out his legs. 'We leave the boat and walk around—yes?'

'Leave the boat?' Alexandra's mouth felt dry. 'And—walk through the jungle?'

'For short distance only.'

'I see.'

'You will need these men to carry your cases.'

'And—and the boat?'

'It is hauled along the river-bank above the rapids.'

'I—didn't realise.' Another anxiety, Alexandra thought sickly, contemplating in imagination the scores of insects and snakes they might encounter in the forest. She had an intense and cowardly desire to turn back.

'And—we sleep in the boat, is that right?'

'Safest,' nodded Santos, chewing at the end of his cigar, and while she pondered this he turned and shouted: '*Maria!*' at the top of his voice. When the Indian girl appeared, he grasped her familiarly about her hips, dragging her close against him and saying: 'You tell that *inutil* Vasco I want to see him, yes?'

Maria pulled away and went to do his bidding while Alexandra poured herself another cup of coffee. She wished she smoked. Right now she would have appreciated something to calm her nerves. On her first evening she had sampled some of Santos's spirit alcohol in an impulsive effort to appear sophisticated, but she had spent several hours afterwards being violently sick and she had not repeated the experience. Indeed, she had avoided almost everything, food as well as drink, that did not come out of a tin and in consequence she had avoided any further gastric disturbances.

But now she could have done with some stimulating brew to dispel the sense of chilling apprehension she was feeling.

Vasco arrived with Maria, looking more than ever like a monkey as he loped along beside her. He had long arms and a short body, and a shaggy mat of black hair which Alexandra supposed he must comb but which never looked as though he had. She felt an hysterical sense of the ridiculous overwhelming her. To think—she had left the comfort of an exclusive boarding school, or the equally exclusive luxury of her father's house in a fashionable square in London, to live in a mud hut in the heart of the Amazonian rain forest. She must be *mad*!

Santos's conversation with Vasco was conducted in Portuguese and Alexandra understood little of it. But what did emerge was that Santos had accused the other man of delaying here because he was paid by the day and the longer he took to deliver Alexandra to her destination the more money he made. Until then Alexandra had hardly considered that aspect of it, and somehow just talking about money made everything seem a little more normal.

The wrangle continued, but Alexandra turned her attention to the river. In truth, it looked very little different today than it had done the day before, but for all his obesity and his disgusting affair with Maria, she trusted Santos more than the wizened Vasco. She half wished it was he, and not the other man, who was to escort her on the final leg of her journey.

Eventually Vasco went away muttering to himself but apparently persuaded that the waters were subsiding. Santos sat, smiling and nodding, and when Alexandra looked at him, he said:

'You will go now, Mees Tempest. Santos will see you on your way.'

'You mean—we're leaving today?' Alexandra was surprised to find how little enthusiasm this aroused in her now that the moment had actually come. Although perhaps after her anxiety earlier she could be forgiven for losing the determination with which she had initially begun this journey.

'Is right,' agreed Santos, lighting another cigar from the stub of the first. 'Santos will see that you have everything you need.'

Alexandra got to her feet. 'I'd better get my things——'

Santos yelled for Maria, and when she came he told her to go and collect the *senhorita*'s cases from her hut. Alexandra began to protest that she was perfectly capable of getting her own things, but Santos interrupted her, saying:

'Maria will do it. Leave her. The Indians like to serve. Hadn't you noticed?'

Alexandra made no response to this. If she had she might have been tempted to tell Santos exactly what she thought of the kind of servitude in which he held Maria, and she had no wish to make enemies here. So she merely smiled and walked to the edge of the landing, looking down in to the amazingly clear waters of the Velhijo. She could see the sandy bottom lying beneath the water, the bleached rocks and curious dark red tinging of the water in places which from a distance made it appear almost black. She realised it was the mineral deposits in the river, swept down by the force of the elements, and it was mostly iron which gave it its curious colour. On the opposite bank, what had appeared to be a log moved, and she saw to her horror that it was one

14

of the grey alligators, called caymans, which she had seen from time to time on the river-bank on her journey to Los Hermanos. Its narrow beady eyes and raised nostrils which enabled it to swim almost completely submerged sent a shiver of apprehension up her spine and she took an involuntary step backward. What would they do if they encountered something like that as they tramped past the rapids? She had little confidence in Vasco's protection.

But by the time the boat was loaded with sleeping bags and extra blankets, cans of water and supplies, and two rifles had been added to the pile of equipment in the bottom of the boat, she felt a little more relaxed. The two Indians who were to accompany them seemed cheerful enough, although Alexandra had to avert her eyes from their apparent disregard for clothing of any sort. They sat together in the prow of the boat, chewing the tobacco which had blackened their teeth, and talking in some language of their own. She tried not to think about the fact that apart from Vasco's, theirs were to be the only other human faces she was likely to see for two whole days. She had too much imagination, she decided.

Santos waved them off. He had shown little surprise at her adventurous journey to see her father, and Alexandra could only assume that like the Indians he considered all white people slightly eccentric. And, too, he had displayed little interest in her destination, and she hoped this was not because he never expected her to reach it.

A bend in the river hid the trading post from view and the boat's small motor chugged steadily upstream. There was a canvas canopy rigged at the rear end of the craft and Alexandra sat beneath this, glad of the respite from the glare of the sun which was just beginning to make the heat unbearable. In fact, it was a little better on the river. There was a slight breeze as the boat moved through the water, and Alexandra fanned herself with her sunglasses.

Well, she thought, trying to be philosophical, she was at least moving again, and who knows, maybe in less than forty-eight hours she would see her father again. It seemed an unreal supposition.

They didn't stop at lunch-time, but Vasco chewed a hunk of the mandioca bread and drank some beer while Alexandra opened a tin of Coke and peeled two bananas. The fresh fruit was infinitely more delicious than any she had tasted in England, and if the Coke was a little warm, it couldn't be helped. The Indians had nothing to eat, but grabbed the tins of beer Vasco threw to them with eager fingers, tearing open the tops and drinking greedily, the liquid dripping out of the corners of their mouths in their haste. Alexandra tried not to watch them, aware that her interest might be misconstrued, but their behaviour both repelled and fascinated her.

She fell asleep after lunch. She had not intended to do so, but she slept so fitfully at night that it was almost impossible to stay awake during the heat of the day. She was awakened by the sound of an aircraft overhead, but by the time she had pulled herself together it had disappeared. At least the intense heat had lessened somewhat, and she had been long enough in the river-basin to know that at night it could be bitterly cold. She yawned and stretched her legs, turning up the trouser cuffs to allow the air to get at her bare legs, and then rolled them down again at the awareness of having an audience.

Late in the afternoon, Vasco turned off the boat's engine and secured the craft to the jutting stump of a long dead tree by the means of a thick rope. 'We stay,' he announced, mainly for Alexandra's benefit. 'Go on—*amanha*.'

'Tomorrow?' Alexandra licked her dry lips. 'Couldn't we go a little further today?'

Vasco shook his head. '*Rapidos, senhorita. Nao caminho!*'

Alexandra wished she had a Portuguese phrase book. She

16

had the distinct suspicion that Vasco knew more English than he let on. It made it simpler for him if she couldn't argue with him.

Now she was forced to acquiesce, and watched with astonishment as the two Indians dived over the side to swim and play in the water. Alexandra was almost sure there were piranhas in the river and she waited in horror for something terrible to happen. But nothing did. The two Indians swam to the river-bank, climbed ashore, and soon began gathering twigs to make a fire.

Dragging her attention from them, Alexandra became aware that Vasco was rigging up a kind of fishing line. He dangled it over the side, and before too long he caught an enormous fish, hauling it in and killing it mercilessly.

'*Tucunare!*' observed Vasco, with evident satisfaction. 'You like?'

Alexandra shook her head vigorously. 'No, thank you,' she declined politely. A tin of beans or corned beef might be less appetising, but definitely safer. Even so, when Vasco started a fire in a kind of brazier and barbecued the fish he had caught, the smell was irresistible. It was almost dark by this time, and the towering trees around them seemed to be pressing in on them. Alexandra felt very much alone, and when Vasco again proffered some of the fish she found herself accepting.

It was absolutely delicious, and Alexandra ate ravenously, enjoying it more than anything she had had since leaving Manaus eight days ago. Licking her fingers afterwards, she looked towards the river-bank and saw the glow of the fire the Indians had lighted. Seemingly they did not find the forest frightening, and were equally capable of providing for themselves when it came to food.

Vasco doused the fire and lighted a lamp. Then he sat cross-legged in the bottom of the boat, poking his teeth with a sliver of wood. Alexandra wished he would stare at

17

something else instead of her all the time, but as he had been kind enough to provide her with a delicious supper perhaps she ought to try and behave naturally.

'Do—er—do you have any children, Vasco?' she ventured tentatively.

The wizened face grimaced. '*Filhos? Nao, senhorita.*' He pointed to his face. '*Me? Me—repugnante!* Who like Vasco?'

Alexandra felt a surge of compassion. 'Why—why, that's nonsense, Vasco. I—I'm sure there are lots—of girls who would be—be proud to marry you.'

Vasco's eyes narrowed to slits. 'You theenk so?' he asked, shuffling a little nearer to her.

Alexandra quelled the urge to shift her legs from out of his reach. 'I—I'm sure of it.'

'And you, *senhorita*? You have *muitos namorados, sim*?'

Alexandra understood what this meant. 'I—I have boy-friends, yes,' she admitted.

'*Naturalmente*, the *senhorita esta muita formosa*!'

Alexandra gave what she hoped was a deprecatory smile and forced a glance towards the camp-fire glowing among the trees on the bank. 'The—the—er—Indians seem quite at home in the forest, don't they?' she said hurriedly.

'Is their home,' replied Vasco, without interest. 'Tell me, *senhorita*, tell me about your boy-friends, *sim*? Do they touch you? Do they—make love to you?'

Alexandra was revolted by the perversion of his curiosity. Pressing her lips together, she said coldly: 'Where are you going to sleep, *senhor*?'

Vasco was unperturbed. 'Where would the *senhorita* like Vasco to sleep?'

Alexandra gasped. 'I—I beg your pardon?'

Vasco got to his knees, grasping her ankles with horny fingers. 'The *senhorita* need not be afraid with Vasco,' he said, his English improving all the time. 'Vasco will not leave you alone.'

'The *senhorita* is not afraid,' snapped Alexandra, struggling to free her ankles, and trying to squash the feeling of panic that was rising inside her. 'Please let go of me, or—or——'

'Or what will you do?' Vasco's face twisted into the semblance of a smile. 'Will you shout for help? From whom? Who can hear you here?' He flicked a contemptuous glance towards the Indians' fire. 'They? *Nao.* They would like to take their turn.'

'You're—you're disgusting!'

Alexandra wrenched her feet out of his hands and lunged to one side. She had no clear idea of what she was about to do. Diving into the river or escaping into the forest were two equally impossible alternatives, but she had to do something or she would scream. She fell against the equipment in the well of the boat and something scraped painfully along her hip. It was a rifle.

Grasping it like a lifeline, she swung round on her knees pointing the barrel towards Vasco. 'If—if you move, I'll shoot!' she declared in a ridiculously tremulous voice, but Vasco sat back on his heels and roared with laughter. 'I—I mean it,' she added fiercely. 'I have used a gun before.'

'Have you, *senhorita*?' Vasco shook his head. '*Veja*—you have me in fear and trembling!' And he held out one hand and deliberately shook it in front of her face.

Exactly what Vasco might have done next Alexandra was never to know, because almost simultaneously they heard the sound of an engine throbbing on the still night air. It was a boat coming down-stream, Alexandra thought, and her heart leapt and then subsided again. What now?

Sounds carried a tremendous distance in the uncanny silence of this watery maze and it was some time before the craft appeared round the bend in the river. There were lights on board and the sound of men's voices, but it was

19

impossible to tell yet what language they were speaking. Alexandra sat in frozen apprehension, hardly aware of the rifle still in her hands.

The occupants of the other boat saw them. It would have been impossible for them not to have seen the light of the lamp, and Alexandra tensed as the craft drew nearer. It was a smaller vessel and a tall man was profiled near its bow, standing looking towards them, saying something to the other men in the boat as it drew alongside. Then he hailed Alexandra's companion:

'*Bem*, Vasco, *tu velho patife, como esta?*'

The boats ground gently together and the other craft's motor was cut as Vasco scrambled to his feet, completely disregarding the possible menace of the rifle Alexandra was holding.

A stream of Portuguese issued from his throat as he greeted the stranger, shaking his hand warmly as the other man vaulted into their boat, glancing back at Alexandra and then continuing to talk excitedly.

Alexandra got unsteadily to her feet, holding on to the rifle. If this man was a friend of Vasco's, what possible assistance could she expect from him? She stared intently at him. It was impossible to distinguish his features as he was still in the shadows, but his height seemed to negate his being an Indian. He kept turning his head in her direction, however, and she wondered with increasing alarm whether he imagined she was easy game, too.

Eventually he seemed to take command, for he silenced Vasco with an unmistakable gesture and then stepped across the pile of equipment in the bottom of the boat into the light.

Alexandra took a step backward, her eyes widening as she realised he looked almost European. He was deeply tanned, of course; no one could be otherwise who lived in this area, and his hair was very dark and longer than Vasco's, but his lean, harshly arrogant features and thin mouth were almost patrician in cast. Even so, there was a certain sinuous quality about the way he moved that few Europeans possessed, and his eyes were amazingly as pale as blue fire. He was a handsome brute, Alexandra had to concede that, and from the way his eyes were assessing her with almost insolent appraisal he was perfectly aware of it.

'*Boa tarde, senhorita!*' he greeted her politely, with a faint but perceptible bow of his head, which went rather oddly with the close-fitting denim pants he was wearing and the denim shirt which was opened almost to his waist. 'Isn't that rifle a little heavy for you?'

He spoke English without any trace of an accent, and Alexandra stared at him in amazement. Her fingers slackened for a moment round the rifle and then tightened again.

'Who are you?' she demanded tautly.

The stranger cast a mocking glance back at Vasco, and then, while Alexandra was off guard, he stepped forward and twisted the rifle effortlessly out of her hands. 'That's better, is it not?' he enquired, examining the weapon expertly. 'Now—as to who I am, I suggest you tell me your name first.'

Alexandra was rubbing her fingers where his determined removal of the rifle had grazed them, and she stared at him a trifle desperately. 'Look,' she said unsteadily, 'I don't see why I have to tell you anything. I—I—this man here——'

'Who? Vasco?'

'Yes, Vasco. He—he was threatening me.'

'*Nao!*' Vasco was openly indignant. 'I did not have *espingarda, senhorita* . . .'

The stranger ignored the other man's outburst and went on calmly: 'With what was he threatening you?'

Alexandra looked down at her hands. 'I'd really rather not talk about it.'

The stranger's lips twisted sardonically. 'I see.' He

paused. 'A woman—or should I say, a girl?—who is prepared to travel unescorted must be prepared to look after herself.' He tossed the rifle carelessly back to her and she managed to catch it before it fell on the deck at her feet. 'Look at it,' he commanded. 'Not only is it not loaded, but the safety catch is still on.'

Alexandra looked rather warily down at the gun in her hands. She had never handled a rifle before this evening, not any gun if it came to that, in spite of her vain boast to Vasco. And if this man had known that, Vasco, with his awareness of its lack of bullets, must have known it, too.

'Please,' she said, suddenly feeling that it was all too much for her. 'Just go away and leave me alone.'

The stranger dropped the butt of his cigar over the side of the boat and she heard the faint plop as it hit the water and was extinguished. Then he leant forward and removed the rifle from her unresisting fingers, and stood it against the other equipment beside him.

'I'm afraid I can't do that,' he remarked quietly, folding his arms. 'You see, I came here to find you, Miss Tempest.'

CHAPTER TWO

THERE was a minute of complete silence when all Alexandra could hear was the heavy beating of her own heart. She tried to recollect whether she had heard Vasco mention her name in his initial outburst and then decided he must have done, for how else could this man know who she was? And yet he had said he had come here to find her. It didn't make sense!

'Who are you?' she asked at last, unable to find anything more original to say.

'My name is Declan O'Rourke, Miss Tempest. Vasco will vouch for that, I am sure. I live—some distance up-river.'

Declan O'Rourke!

Alexandra felt more than ever confused. Apart from the pale blue eyes between the thick black lashes there was little to indicate his Irish heritage.

'But——' She sought for words. 'How did you know where to find me? And how did you know I was here?'

'Explanations of that sort can wait.' He glanced round at Vasco's expectant face. 'I will escort Miss Tempest from here. You can go back to Los Hermanos and tell Santos——'

'*No!* I mean—wait!' Alexandra bit her lower lip hard. 'How do I know who you are? I mean, you can't just come along and—and take me over!'

'Would you rather stay with Vasco?' O'Rourke's eyes were mocking. 'Did I misunderstand that scene I interrupted?'

'No, no, of course you didn't.' Alexandra wrung her hands. 'But—but you can't expect me to go with you just like that—without any kind of an explanation.'

'I'm afraid you don't have much choice, Miss Tempest,' he returned politely, and she stared impotently at the sweat-stained shoulders of his shirt as he turned away.

Vasco sidled up to him and said something in an under-tone and Alexandra wished desperately that she understood Portuguese. She had no liking for Vasco, nor any real trust, but he had brought her this far. How was she to be sure that this man O'Rourke was not some kind of thief or adven-turer who, the minute they were out of Vasco's sight, would ditch her and take what little money and possessions she had brought with her. Her fingers encountered the narrow gold watch on her wrist. Her father had bought it for her sixteenth birthday just over a year ago, and it was insured for almost two hundred pounds. It, at least, was worth stealing. Perhaps even Vasco was in league with him. Per-haps this was some crooked sort of deal they had cooked up between them.

Declan O'Rourke was beginning to manhandle her suit-cases into the other boat and his actions inspired retaliation. She rushed forward and grasped his arm, preventing him from slinging over the pigskin holdall that contained her heavier clothes. His flesh was hard and warm beneath her fingers, and there were hairs on his arm that roughened the skin. This close she could smell the heat of his body, but it was not an unpleasant smell, and the aroma of tobacco still lingered about him.

He was turning at the moment she grabbed his arm and his elbow caught her in the rib-cage so that she gasped and released him, collapsing awkwardly on to the pile of blank-ets.

'I'm sorry.' There was a faint smile on his face as he

hauled her to her feet at once, making sure she was not hurt by holding her for a moment until she drew free of him. 'That was careless of me. I'm sure you want to help, but I can manage.'

Alexandra glared at him frustratedly. 'You know perfectly well that was not my intention!' she exclaimed. 'Oh —this is ridiculous! What are you doing with my belongings? What do you intend to do with me?'

Declan O'Rourke regarded her mockingly. 'You really don't trust anyone, do you?'

'I haven't had much encouragement!' retorted Alexandra unsteadily, her momentary anger dissipating beneath other anxieties.

'Very well. I—heard—there was a young woman waiting at Los Hermanos, waiting to come to Paradiablo.'

'How did you hear that?'

'You would call it a—grapevine, I think. We have quite an efficient one, believe me.'

'Senhor O'Rourke lives at Paradiablo,' put in Vasco, and was silenced by a piercing look from those chilling blue eyes.

'I see.' Alexandra was trying to make sense of this. 'Do you know my father, Mr. O'Rourke?'

'Professor Tempest? Yes, I know him.'

Alexandra breathed a sigh of relief. 'Then you know he is at Paradiablo, too.'

'Professor Tempest has been working at Paradiablo for several months, yes.'

Alexandra's warm mouth curved into a smile. 'Thank heavens for that! Oh—does he know I'm here, too?'

'No.' Declan O'Rourke sounded quite definite about that. He bent and completed his transference of her belongings to the other boat. Then he straightened. 'I presume you are prepared to come with me now?'

Alexandra hesitated. 'But I thought—oughtn't we to stay

here overnight? Vasco said something about—rapids?'

Declan O'Rourke cast a wry glance in Vasco's direction. 'Did he? Yes—well, there are rapids further upstream, but we will not be negotiating them this evening.'

Alexandra frowned. 'I don't understand.'

'You will.' Declan O'Rourke indicated his boat. 'Do you need any assistance to climb across?'

Alexandra shook her head and then looked uncomfortably towards Vasco. How did he feel about losing his passenger?

'Er—how much—how much do I owe you?' she began.

'I'll attend to that.'

Declan O'Rourke spoke before Vasco's greedy little mouth could voice a figure, and Alexandra had no choice but to leave him to it. She scrambled over into the adjoining boat, flinching away from the Indian hands which reached to help her, and standing rather uneasily in the well of the vessel watching the two men complete their business. She was still not entirely convinced that she was doing the right thing. There were still a lot of questions left unanswered. But she had made her decision and she had no choice but to stick to it.

A few moments later, Declan O'Rourke vaulted back into his own boat again and with a raised hand to Vasco he nodded to his Indian pilot and they began to move away. In no time at all the darkness had sucked them into its waiting void and Alexandra hugged herself closely, huddled on the plank seat, wondering what on earth her father was going to say when she saw him. She had the uneasy conviction that he was not going to be at all pleased.

Declan O'Rourke did not speak to her as the small vessel moved steadily upstream and apart from an occasional word between him and the Indian pilot the only sounds were the slapping movements of the water against the bows of the boat.

26

They travelled for perhaps half an hour and then Alexandra realised they were pulling across to the bank. Her nerves tightened. What now? Was this where they were going to abandon her—to be eaten alive by alligators or crushed to death by the giant anaconda of her nightmares?

The boat crunched against the spongy roots of dead undergrowth, and Declan O'Rourke sprang across on to marshy ground and secured a rope. Then he came back to where Alexandra was sitting and said:

'Have you got boots?' in a curt, uncompromising tone.

Alexandra blinked. 'Boots? Oh—yes, of course.'

'Put them on then. We're going ashore.'

'Ashore?' Alexandra looked in horror at the menacing belt of tropical forest. 'But——'

'Don't argue right now. Just do as I say.'

Declan turned away with the air of one accustomed to command and what was more, accustomed to being obeyed. Alexandra found herself fumbling for her boots and pushing her feet into them. When they were fastened she stood up and Declan came back to her shouldering a load of blankets and carrying a powerful torch.

'Come along,' he said, indicating that she should follow him and with a reluctant look at her belongings strewn in the bottom of the boat she obeyed.

The two Indians who were accompanying him were apparently remaining in the boat and Alexandra forced herself into a fatalistic frame of mind. Whatever happened now, she was powerless to prevent it.

Declan leapt on to the marshy river-bank and lent a hand as she jumped across the lapping shallows to land beside him. Her boots sank into the soggy ground and squelched as Declan switched on the torch and went ahead, urging her to follow him.

There was a path worn through the jungle at this point and it was surprisingly easy walking. Of course, all around

27

them were the poisonous liana creepers that fought their way upward in a strangling spiral round the trunks of trees, and there might be any number of minor monsters underfoot, but Alexandra refused to think of them. The uncanny silence created an illusion of complete isolation, and the thought crossed her mind that these forests had existed here longer than man had peopled the earth. It was a shattering realisation.

An unearthly roar that echoed and re-echoed around them caused Alexandra to gasp and stumble, but she managed to right herself with resorting to clutching at her escort. All the same, she glanced back rather fearfully over her shoulder, half expecting to find a jaguar with dripping jaws panting malevolently behind her, but then her head jerked forward again as her companion said calmly:

'Don't be alarmed. It's miles away. But sound carries in the forest.'

Alexandra nodded, not trusting herself to say anything and then walked into him without realising he had stopped and was pointing to a light a few yards away.

'Our destination,' he observed dryly, propelling her away from him again. 'It belongs to a friend of mine and his family.'

Alexandra's eyes widened. 'You mean—people actually *live* out here?'

'Why not?' His voice had cooled perceptibly.

'But—I mean—how can they?' She spread her hands in an encompassing movement.

He looked down at her and even in the faint light from the torch she could sense his displeasure. 'To live means different things to different people, Miss Tempest. I realise that in your society material things are the criterion by which success in life is judged, but here we have a more basic appreciation of happiness.'

Alexandra coloured and was glad he could not see it. She

28

wanted to retaliate, to tell him that he knew nothing about the kind of society she moved in. How could he, living here in this remote part of the world, the rivers his only link with civilisation? But to stand arguing with him in the middle of the jungle with the darkness of night pressing all around them seemed the height of absurdity, so she remained silent.

He walked away towards the hut from which the light was coming and Alexandra stumbled after him. She was beginning to feel the coldness that came from too much exposure to the damp night air and the shivering that enveloped her was as much to do with that as nervousness. Even so, she was nervous, although her blind panic had left her.

A man emerged from the hut as they approached, carrying a lamp. Alexandra saw to her relief that he was at least wearing a pair of torn, but adequately covering, shorts, although his appearance was not encouraging. His brown Indian features were battered and scarred, and his teeth were blackened by the usual chewing of tobacco root. Behind him clustered his wife and a group of children of varying ages from two to teenage. He greeted Declan O'Rourke as warmly as Vasco had done, but their conversation was conducted in one of the Indian dialects Alexandra had heard since coming to Los Hermanos.

His wife and the children were more interested in Alexandra. Clearly they had seen Declan O'Rourke before, but a white girl was a different matter. Alexandra, shivering in her shirt and jeans, wondered however they managed to keep warm in such a minimum amount of clothing.

They were invited inside. The hut was larger than she had at first imagined, but it soon became apparent that they were all expected to share the same sleeping area. In the light of the lamp, Declan O'Rourke's eyes challenged her to find some fault with this arrangement, and rather than create any unpleasantness Alexandra made no demur. She supposed she ought to feel grateful that she was at least warm again, even though the charcoal fire burning in one corner of the hut filled the air with smoke before escaping out of a hole in the thatched roof, but it was infinitely better than sleeping in the open boat as she had expected to do.

Declan O'Rourke introduced her to their host and his wife, who, although they could not speak her language, made her welcome by smiles and gestures. Their names Alexandra knew she would never remember, but their children, amazingly, had English names, and Declan explained in an undertone that a missionary in the area had converted them to Christianity. In consequence, all the younger children had names taken straight out of the Bible.

The clear spirit which Santos had offered her that first night at Los Hermanos was proffered and when she tried to refuse Declan put the mud-baked utensil into her hands.

'Drink!' he commanded harshly, and she stared at him mutinously.

'I don't like it,' she protested, but his eyes were without sympathy.

'Learn to do so,' he said, swallowing the liquid he had been given with evident relish. 'Or would you like me to force it down your throat?'

Alexandra's lips parted. 'Look, I realise this is an example of their hospitality——'

'Just drink it,' said Declan, with resignation, his eyes hard and unyielding, and with a helpless shrug of her shoulders she raised the cup to her lips.

In fact it wasn't half as bad as she had anticipated. It burned her throat, but it did create a warm glow inside her which banished a little of her tension. Declan O'Rourke spoke to their host while they drank and then after the dishes were cleared away it seemed expected that they should now retire.

The Indian and his family had the usual kind of hammocks to sleep in, and already the children were curling up together with a complete disregard as to age and sex. Declan politely refused the use of the Indian's hammock and spread a ground-sheet over the hard floor, covering it with a blanket. Then he indicated to Alexandra that she should sit down on it.

After a moment's hesitation, Alexandra did as she was silently bidden, and watched in amazement when he came down beside her, spreading the other blankets over their legs.

'Now wait a minute ...' she began, but he interrupted her impatiently.

'This is no time for maidenly modesty, Miss Tempest. In the jungle one abides by the law of survival. What is it they say about Rome and the Romans? Right now, all I'm interested in is getting you safely to Paradiablo, for your father's sake.'

It was the first time he had voluntarily made any mention of their eventual destination, and her spirits rose. But the lamp was extinguished at that moment and only total darkness remained, which disconcerted her again. She felt Declan stretch his length beside her and closed her eyes before moving as far away from him as possible on the rough blanket. She was loath to lie down, to place herself in such a vulnerable position, but she could hardly sit up all night, could she? And besides, what had she to be afraid of?

She lay down cautiously. She had never shared a bed with anyone before, and except at boarding school she had always had a room of her own. Of course, now she was growing older she had thought about sleeping with boys, and at school her girl friends found the topic infinitely interesting. But although she was aware that that sort of thing did go on, she had never allowed her relationships with the opposite sex to get that far. On the contrary, she avoided promiscuous situations, and it was a totally new experience to lie down beside a man.

Her nails curled into her palms. She could imagine the comments she would arouse if she went back to school and told her friends the details of this little expedition. And she would not be exaggerating if she told them that Declan O'Rourke was one of the most attractive men she had ever encountered. Attractive, physically, that is. She was not so sure about his personality. But then she had had little to do with mature men of ... how many years? She frowned. Thirty? She supposed he might be younger. But no doubt the life he led here did not lend itself to lengthening the period of one's existence. On the contrary. Anyone who lived here deserved a medal for endurance, she decided ironically.

She drew the blankets up to her chin. She was cold. In spite of the ground-sheet, the dampness of the earth seemed to strike up at her and she wished she had had the sense to bring a woollen sweater with her from the boat.

Declan O'Rourke stirred. 'Relax,' he mumbled sleepily, misinterpreting her movements. 'I won't touch you. I prefer to sleep alone, but as we have only one ground-sheet ...'

Alexandra rolled on to her side away from him, resenting the fact that he had been the one to voice his dissatisfaction with the situation, and a few moments later she heard his steady breathing. She hunched her shoulders miserably, trying not to shiver. She was not used to the hardness of the floor, or the snuffling sounds coming from one of the smaller children. And there was a catarrhal snore issuing from someone's throat. What an awful place this was, she thought, sniffing. She felt hot tears pressing at her eyelids. It was self-pity, she knew, but she couldn't help it. At least at Los Hermanos she had had a hammock to sleep in, up and away from the possible intrusion of ants or spiders. Oh,

God, she thought sickly, what if a tarantula entered the hut during the night as one had at Los Hermanos? What if it crawled across the blanket on to her face?

She caught her breath on a sob, shuddering uncontrollably, and almost jumped out of her skin when a warm arm curved over her waist, drawing her back against a hard muscular body. She struggled automatically until his mouth beside her ear said rather resignedly:

'I'm not about to rape you, but you are cold—and terrified too, I guess. I'm not completely without sensitivities, you know.'

Alexandra stopped struggling, but she held herself stiffly. 'You said you wouldn't touch me!' she accused him in a whisper.

'You want I should let you go?' His voice had hardened.

All of a sudden Alexandra gave in and relaxed against him. His warmth was enveloping her like a comforting shield, and she no longer wanted to resist him.

'No,' she admitted huskily, overwhelmingly aware of the masculine hardness of his thighs against hers. 'I—I'm sorry. I was frozen!'

His hand on her stomach drew her closer into the curve of his body. 'I can feel that,' he observed quietly. 'Now, I suggest you get some sleep. You're perfectly safe.'

But it was easier said than done. Although she was now warm, she was also disturbed by his nearness. She had never been this close to any man before and she moved against him restlessly, feeling every movement he made.

At last he said: 'For God's sake, lie still, or I won't be responsible for the consequences!' in a curiously rough tone, and the harsh words caused her to·remain motionless until sleep came to claim her.

The sounds of the children woke her. She blinked and opened her eyes warily, and then became conscious of the weight of Declan's arm across her breasts. He was still asleep, she thought, but when she made a tentative move to escape from his hold, his eyes opened and looked into hers. She felt herself flushing. She couldn't help it. But he merely gave her a half mocking smile before rolling on to his back and rubbing his hand over the darkening stubble of his chin.

Alexandra sat up, smoothing a hand over the heavy weight of her hair, feeling its tangled disorder. The hut door was open and the children were running in and out. The wife of their host was sitting in one corner of the hut suckling the youngest child at her drooping breasts, while from outside came the smell of food roasting over a fire. She looked down at Declan, as relaxed as if he had just spent the night in a comfortable bed, and her colour deepened again as his eyes moved to the rounded outline of her breasts beneath the thin material of her blouse.

'You'd better button your shirt,' he remarked dryly. 'Women's Lib may be all right for the natives, but I don't somehow think you're that emancipated.'

Alexandra's lips parted and she looked down in embarrassment to find a couple of the buttons of her blouse had become unfastened during the night. Her fingers fumbled them into their holes and then she got to her feet, brushing down her denim jeans in an effort to assure herself that they at least were decent.

Declan sat up, running his fingers through the thickness of his straight hair. 'There are no washing facilities here,' he said, 'but you can wash in the river if you wish. As to the other ...' he grinned, 'there are plenty of trees for cover.'

Alexandra gave him an impatient look and then walked to the door of the hut. Outside their host was spit-roasting something over his fire. It looked like meat and it smelt like meat, but when Declan came to stand behind her he said it was fish. Alexandra ate some, sitting cross-legged like

Declan, and found it amazingly good. Or maybe it was that she had had so little to eat the day before, anything would have tasted good.

After the meal, Declan collected the blankets and they bade their hosts goodbye. Then they walked back through the jungle to the river where the boat was rocking gently on its mooring. Declan slung the blankets into the boat and then began unbuttoning his shirt and trousers. Alexandra stared at him in alarm.

'What are you doing?' she exclaimed in horror.

Declan threw off his shirt and with a mild grimace examined a tick which had embedded itself on his chest during the night. Then he bent to take off his trousers, saying: 'I'm going for a swim. Want to join me?'

'*In the river!*' Alexandra gasped. 'But aren't there piranhas in the water?'

'Probably,' he agreed, looking down at the purple trunks which were his only piece of underwear. Then he smiled. 'I won't horrify you by stripping to the raw. But I don't mind if you do.'

Alexandra shook her head, turning away apprehensively as he dived cleanly into the water, and then glanced back over her shoulder, half expecting him to appear minus a limb. However, he came up, shaking his hair back out of his eyes, and swam across the current with powerful strokes.

Alexandra remained on the bank until he emerged unscathed, brushing the water from his body and drying himself with one of the blankets thrown to him by the Indians in the boat.

'That's better,' he said, reaching for his pants and pulling them on over the wet trunks. 'Are you sure you wouldn't like to try it?'

'No, thank you.' Alexandra watched him covertly, noticing how broad his shoulders were and how the muscles of his chest rippled beneath the curls of black hair. There was

35

hair on his stomach, too, but she found him watching her and quickly looked away. Even so, she was aware that she was trembling a little, and her heart pounded loudly in her ears. She had never felt this way before, and she told herself severely that it was the complete lack of inhibition around here that caused the moistening of her palms and the curious weakening sensation in the pit of her stomach. She was not used to seeing half-naked men, or women either if it came to that.

'You'd better check that you don't have any bugs making their home beneath your skin,' he advised, leaving the top buttons of his shirt unfastened and tucking the bottom into his pants with no apparent sense of embarrassment at her scrutiny.

'Bugs?' Alexandra stared at him.

'Bugs, ticks—what's the difference? You don't leave them alone. Want me to look?'

'*No!*' Alexandra was horrified. Shaking her head vigorously, she turned away, and unbuttoned her blouse, examining her breasts for any horrible little insects like the tick he had flicked off his own chest. But to her relief there was nothing to be seen and she was about to fasten her blouse again when her fingers brushed against something warm and bulging fastened to the skin that covered her diaphragm. With a little gasp she twisted herself to see what it was and almost fainted when she realised it was a leech.

'Oh, God!' she moaned, and at once he was beside her, jerking her round to face him, his eyes darkening when he saw what it was that had caused her despair.

'Don't panic,' he muttered, going down on his haunches and taking out his knife. 'Now—I'll try not to hurt you, but *keep still!*'

Alexandra nodded, her fists clenched. She felt the stinging pain as the revolting creature dropped to the ground, and then Declan leant forward and put his mouth to the place where it had been, sucking hard. That hurt, more than the removal of the worm had done, but she stood motionless until he spat away the blood he had drawn and rose to his feet. Then, with trembling fingers, she gathered her blouse protectively about her and burst into tears.

Declan studied her woebegone face with wry compassion. Then he said: 'It's not as bad as all that, you know. But hang on. I've got some antiseptic in my kit. I think it needs something over it.'

He swung himself across and into the boat, and came back a few minutes later with a bottle and an elastic plaster. The antiseptic stung abominably, but Alexandra was too distraught to protest.

However, by the time he had secured the plaster and buttoned her blouse for her she was beginning to feel a little ashamed of her outburst. She rubbed her eyes with the backs of her hands, smearing dust across her cheeks.

'I suppose you think I'm a fool,' she said.

Declan shook his head. 'Why should I think that? It was a normal reaction. Better to get it over with than bottling it up. I thought you behaved rather well in the circumstances. At least you didn't scream when I used the knife.'

Alexandra bit hard on her lower lip. 'Will it—I mean, it's not poisonous or anything, is it?'

Declan pushed her gently but firmly towards the boat. 'No. You'll survive. But I'll have another look at it tonight, if you've no objections?'

Alexandra hunched her shoulders. 'There's not much point in objecting now, is there?'

Declan helped her into the boat. 'My dear child, the sight of the naked female form is no novelty around here, believe me!' An amused quirk to his mouth made her feel rather silly and unsophisticated. 'And besides, you've got a beautiful body. Why be ashamed of it? You'll have to shed those stupid trivial inhibitions if you want to enjoy your time out here.'

Her terror was subsiding and Alexandra felt more annoyed than anything. Annoyed with herself for giving in to blind panic, and annoyed with him for assuming that because he lived here its ways necessarily had to be acceptable to all.

'If you imagine you can persuade me to go native, Mr. O'Rourke, you're mistaken,' she declared shortly.

His expression was derisive. 'I wouldn't dream of suggesting such a thing, Miss Tempest.' His lips twisted. 'But don't make the mistake of thinking that these people would be interested, either way. We may not be as—*civilised*—as you like to think you are, but at least we don't have a percentage of the population getting their kicks from leering at lewd books, or getting hot under the collar watching some female take off her clothes! And if you stripped here and now, you'd arouse nothing more than a mild curiosity! Your white skin isn't at all appealing to them.'

'I suppose you're going to tell me that Vasco——'

Declan gave her an impatient look and then nodded to the pilot that they were ready to cast off. 'Vasco is a mulatto, and as far as I know he has no Indian blood in his veins. Besides, I've no doubt he was only trying to frighten you. You're a little young and inexperienced for his tastes!'

Alexandra clenched her lips tightly together and turned sideways on the plank seat away from him. It seemed that whatever she said he was always able to take control of the conversation. She stared impotently towards the mist rising from the trees on the opposite bank. The mornings could be quite beautiful, but she didn't appreciate that now. All she could think was that the sooner they reached Paradiablo, and her father, the better she would like it.

CHAPTER THREE

AFTER about half an hour Alexandra began to hear the sound of rushing water and her nerve ends tingled as she realised they must be approaching the rapids Vasco had spoken about. Declan O'Rourke had said nothing more to her and had seated himself in the forward part of the boat where he could talk to the Indians. He had lit a cigar and looked completely at his ease. Obviously the rapids held no fears for him.

She sighed. She couldn't help but envy his composure. Nothing seemed to disconcert him. He was at home here as the Indians themselves. He shared their food, their homes, their conversation. He swam in their rivers with a complete disregard for the dangers of piranhas and alligators, as they did, while she . . .

She shook her head. It was an unfair comparison. She was English. She had had a comparatively sheltered up-bringing. Just because he chose to live in some dank hole in the forest it did not mean that his way was best. Perhaps he had never had the opportunity to do anything else. No doubt her father had a totally different outlook.

Her father!

She cupped her chin in her hands. Surely he wouldn't be angry with her for making this journey. Surely he would see that she had only done it because she loved him and wanted to be with him, wouldn't he? She frowned, remembering occasions when as a child she had disobeyed him in the past. He wasn't always the most even-tempered of men, and it was quite possible that he would demand that she return home to England immediately.

She squared her shoulders. Well, she wasn't a child now. She was seventeen. She would be eighteen soon. At eighteen one acquired maturity, it was said. So what difference did a few months make?

They inevitably reached that stretch of the river where the water churned and bubbled over ugly black rocks that reared their heads above the spume. Alexandra sat on the edge of her seat, waiting for them to pull over to the side. But they didn't.

The Indians produced paddles, the engine was switched off, and the boat was manhandled through the swirling torrent. Alexandra held the wooden seat so tightly that the wood bit into her fingers, but she was so intent on their negotiation of the rapids that she scarcely felt the self-inflicted pain. Declan O'Rourke had a paddle, too, and inch by inch they climbed the dangerous hissing cauldron until they finally thrust themselves into the comparatively smooth waters above.

A weak sigh escaped her as the paddles were put away and the engine was re-started, but she saw to her surprise that no one else seemed the least concerned. Declan left the Indians and came back to where she was sitting, looking down at her with mocking eyes.

'Well?' he said. 'Did you enjoy that?'

She made an involuntary gesture. 'You must know I didn't.'

'No? I'd have thought you'd have appreciated the excitement.'

Alexandra brushed an insect off her knee. 'Santos said—we would have to walk round the rapids.'

'Did he? Yes, well, that does happen on the longer stretches. This was comparatively simple to negotiate.' He glanced round. 'Not much further now,' he added with

40

satisfaction.

Alexandra clasped her hands. 'Isn't it?' She made a little movement of her shoulders. 'Thank heavens for that!'

Declan seemed about to say something else and then thought better of it. With another wry raising of his dark eyebrows, he turned and went back to his earlier position.

Towards midday, when the heat was becoming intense again, Declan brought the boat in to the bank. To Alexandra's inexperienced eyes it seemed that they had reached nowhere in particular. There was not even a landing, only a cleared pathway through the trees. Was Paradiablo to be a clearing in the forest like that hut they had stayed at the night before? Alexandra's heart sank.

Declan moored the craft and collected his haversack and her cases from the bottom of the boat. The Indians climbed ashore, too, this time and took charge of the heavier luggage. Declan helped Alexandra on to the river-bank and then indicated that she should follow the Indians along the path between the trees. An enormous black bird, about the size of a game bird back home, rose out of the underbrush in front of them, squawking frighteningly, and Alexandra had to be urged onward as her footsteps began to lag.

Presently, however, they emerged into a wide clearing where some attempt at cultivation had been made. There was a small mandioca plantation, and the beginnings of a crop of what might be sweet potatoes, tilled no doubt by the occupants of the collection of huts that edged the forest and who had come out to observe the newcomers. But what attracted Alexandra's instant attention was not the unexpectedly thriving community, or the remarkably good looks of the children, but a gleaming silver aircraft standing on a mudbaked strip.

She swung round to look at Declan with uncomprehending eyes. 'Is that—are we to—fly?'

He half smiled. 'I'm afraid so.'

A faint measure of comprehension came to her. 'Yesterday—there was an aircraft flying around. Was that you?'

Declan nodded. 'The Velhijo is quite a long river. I didn't just happen upon you, if that's what you mean. These men——' He indicated the Indians who had been his crew. 'They come from this village. It's useful for me to have transport to reach Los Hermanos. There is no landing strip there.'

Suddenly it was all beginning to make sense, but still she hesitated. 'Do we—have much further to go, then?'

'About three hundred miles,' he stated calmly, and she gasped.

'But that would have taken *days* by boat!' she protested. 'Didn't you know that?'

'*No!*' She shook her head dazedly. 'Santos was always very vague when I asked about the length of the journey.'

'I'll bet he was.' Declan pushed her forward. 'Go on! The head man of the village is waiting to greet us.'

They were invited to share a meal with the community before continuing their journey and Alexandra looked rather uneasily at Declan when he explained this.

'Don't worry,' he remarked dryly, as rush mats were spread out for their use. 'You won't get food poisoning.'

In fact the meal of roasted venison was remarkably enjoyable and Declan explained that they were honoured in being offered meat. The forests were not teeming with game, and the Indians' main source of protein came from fish.

Afterwards they were escorted to the aircraft and Alexandra felt a surge of excitement as Declan loaded their luggage and helped her inside. It was a beautiful little machine and she wondered to whom it belonged. There was room for the pilot and three passengers and Delcan strapped her into the seat directly behind his.

'All right?' he enquired, levering himself behind the controls, and she nodded eagerly.

'Okay. Here we go!'

Declan put on headphones and Alexandra heard the crackle of static as he contacted air control at Manaus. There was a brief interchange of Portuguese and then the powerful little engine sprang to life sending the propellers spinning wildly. Declan released his brakes and taxied slowly to the end of the narrow runway and then turned to make the take-off.

It was a hair-raising experience. The trees seemed to be rushing towards them as they sped down the strip and Alexandra was convinced they would never clear those towering canopies of leaves. But just as she was closing her eyes, sure that her end had come, the small aircraft lifted and surged upward and over effortlessly. She breathed a sigh of relief and Declan glanced round at her.

'You're going to give yourself heart trouble before you're thirty if you don't stop anticipating the worst,' he remarked, turning back to his observation of the open sky ahead of them. 'You don't suppose that's the first time I've lifted off there, do you?'

Alexandra felt weak. 'No, I suppose not. It was just—all those trees!'

Declan cleared himself with air control and pushed back the headphones. 'You're a mass of nerves,' he said callously. 'I don't know what they teach you at that school of yours, but it surely isn't helping you none.'

Alexandra looked down at the thick carpet of trees below them, intersected by the winding maze of rivers. She marvelled that anyone could navigate the area without getting totally lost. There seemed few landmarks that she could see and even fewer signs of habitation. But it was possible from the air to see the undulations in the landscape and the *varzea* lakes she had read about, trapped in the folds of the hills after the flooding of recent weeks. She was trying not

43

to let what he had said upset her. They were almost to their destination, and the last thing she wanted was for her father to find them hostile towards one another. She had still to discover who this man was, what his occupation was, and exactly how well he knew her father.

They flew low over one of the larger lakes and Alexandra tensed again until Declan said: 'Can you see the herons on the shore there? They nest in the trees at night. It's quite an unusual sight.'

'They have such long legs!' she exclaimed, quite forgetting her earlier annoyance, and Declan nodded.

'I imagine they consider the safety of the upper branches worth the effort,' he commented dryly, and eased back on the stick so that the small plane rose higher again.

Clouds were lowering ahead of them, and Alexandra wondered where they would eventually land. At least it was cool up here, away from the moist heat of the valley floor, and had it not been for the tropical forest beneath them they could have been almost anywhere.

'I think we're going into rough weather,' Declan said suddenly, as his headphones crackled and he lifted them to hear what was being relayed. 'There's a pretty bad storm up ahead, but it isn't forcing aircraft down yet, so I'm going to try and beat it in.'

Alexandra's mouth felt dry, but she refused to let him know how terrified she felt. Instead, she concentrated steadily on the back of his head and when the first purple streak of lightning came out of the leaden sky she hardly flinched. The worst thing of all was the rain which fell in a grey unyielding sheet, obliterating everything beneath its savage shroud. Declan flew on steadily, sometimes taking them a little higher when the small craft was buffeted by the wind that swept and swirled around them, and the noise was deafening. Alexandra had never in her life experienced anything so frightening.

But as quickly as it had appeared, the storm cleared away leaving a washed blue canopy above them. Declan glanced round at her, noticing the paleness of her cheeks and the quivering of her lips, but all he said was: 'Not much further now. Tighten your belt. I'm taking her down.'

Below them the character of the land had changed. There were still trees and rivers, but it was a much hillier area, and Alexandra realised they were in the foothills of the mountains.

She couldn't help the way her heart leapt into her mouth as they skimmed the treetops on the slopes of rocky hillside and closed her eyes as they came in to land on what appeared to be little more than a shelf projecting from the mountainside. She opened her eyes at the feeling of solid ground beneath the plane and saw that in fact it was a tiny airport with white-painted buildings and a proper airstrip.

Declan taxied up to the buildings and after a final word with airport control, took off the headphones. He undid his safety belt and then turned, saying: 'You can stop praying. We're here!' in lazily derisive tones.

Alexandra refused to look at him, busying herself with unfastening her seat belt, and he shrugged before swinging open the door and climbing out. Immediately, a dark-skinned man wearing oil-stained overalls came over to him, shaking his hand and engaging him in conversation and Alexandra was left to make her own arrangements.

Thrusting her legs forward, she grasped the door frame and levered herself out of her seat. Then she turned and slowly climbed down on to the tarmac.

But the effects of the journey had been greater than she had imagined. As her feet touched the ground everything—the plane, the airport buildings, even Declan O'Rourke and the man talking to him—began to spin round dizzily and a wave of nausea swept over her. She pressed a hand weakly to her throat and saw the recognition of her symptoms in

Declan's eyes. She turned away, only just in time. She was violently, and ignominiously, sick, just behind the plane.

She wanted to die, she thought miserably. How could she ever face him again? She rested one hand against the fuselage and felt the world begin to subside once more.

'Take it easy!' Declan's hands descended on her shoulders and his voice was almost gentle. 'You've had a pretty rough day. Come on! The station wagon's over here.'

Alexandra wanted to draw away from him, to show him that she didn't need his pity, but there was something infinitely reassuring about his arm across her shoulders. The man in the white overalls had tactfully moved away, but at a word of command from Declan he hurried forward to unload their gear from the plane.

As they walked towards a dust-smeared station wagon parked at the edge of the strip, Alexandra got a brief impression of the accuracy which must have been needed to land here. In the cool aftermath of the storm the air was fresh and clear for miles, and she could see how the thickly foliaged sward fell away to the right into the river basin. To their left rose the granite-hard slopes of the mountains, reaching up to form jagged peaks against the skyline. Even the mountains had an alien quality about them, a remoteness, as if they felt secure within their walls of impenetrable forest.

But now Declan was swinging open the door of the station wagon and helping her inside, and she felt a sense of relief at the normality of it all after the holocaust she had just experienced. Declan went back to help the other man with their luggage and presently it was stowed in the back of the vehicle and he had bidden the man goodbye. He swung open his own door and climbed in beside her, casting a speculative glance in her direction before starting the motor.

'How do you feel?' he enquired, and she endeavoured to

46

appear composed.

'I'm all right, thank you.'

'Not feeling sick again?'

Alexandra pressed her lips together. 'Must you bring that up?'

A smile lifted the corners of his mouth. 'I thought that was your prerogative!'

Alexandra made an involuntary exclamation. 'Must you always score points, Mr. O'Rourke?'

He flicked the ignition. 'Don't make it so easy for me.'

The station wagon began to move, and determining not to argue with him, Alexandra tried to pay attention to her surroundings. Her stomach did still feel rather queasy, but she wasn't going to give him that satisfaction. She had a strong suspicion that it was all due to that revolting liquid he had made her drink the night before, but such an accusation would be bound to arouse further derision, so she said nothing.

It was late afternoon already and the sun had lost most of its venom. Here in the mountains the air was much cooler anyway, and the breeze coming through the open windows was most refreshing. The track that led away from the small air-strip was nothing more than a series of muddy potholes after the storm, and as it was no wider than the width of the station wagon, Alexandra lived in fear of their meeting another vehicle head-on. It was hair-raising enough driving on the very edge of a precipice which fell away to the river basin below them without the added hazard of tyres skidding on the slippery surface.

However, after a while Alexandra gave herself up to the realisation that nothing she could do would improve matters and therefore, as Declan had pointed out earlier, there was no sense in quickening her heartbeats by puerile panic. The trees and shrubs that sprawled up the mountainside were recognisable as pines and gorse bushes, and once there was the spectacular sight of a carpet of gentians and amaryllis growing beside a tumbling waterfall. It was such an unexpected scene that she could not stifle the gasp of delight that escaped her, and for a moment she forgot her own discomforts in the pure delight of discovery.

'It's not all the ugliness and deprivation you imagined, is it?' observed Declan wryly, glancing sideways at her. 'Here one can pass through all the seasons in a single day. Flowers blossom, wither and die all in the space of twenty-four hours.'

'How sad!' She caught her breath.

'Not necessarily. Who decides the length of a life's span? For man—beast—or plant? Would you gather them and put them in a vase and allow them to eke out an existence in a totally alien environment just so that you could appreciate their beauty a little longer?'

Alexandra frowned. 'You make it sound selfish.'

'Isn't it? Do you honestly believe that you can artificially extend the life of anything if such an undertaking were not ordained?'

'What are you saying? That you don't believe in operations, transfusions—transplants, even?'

'No.' He shook his head. 'I'm no purist. On the contrary, I find such techniques extremely interesting. But that's your environment, your life, your expectation of deliverance. From the minute you're born you are programmed to accept that kind of environment. But everything, every person, has a different programme, and I don't believe you should attempt to impose your life style on anyone else just because you believe in it implicitly.'

Alexandra was intrigued, in spite of herself, and his conversation had had the effect of temporarily banishing her nausea. 'I suppose what you mean is—let nature take its course. Let human nature develop at its own pace. But surely, if you believe this, there would never have been any progress made in technological things.'

'On the contrary, progress is an inborn capacity. It is not cultivated.'

Alexandra shook her head. 'I think that some people need assistance ...'

'Do you? Why?' His thick lashes shaded his eyes. 'Are you so convinced that what you want is right? And what's it all for anyway? Do you realise that those forests down there have existed for a hundred million years? Can you grasp that? Can your puny mind encompass the limitlessness of such a span? I doubt it. It would be impossible. We all tend to imagine that our lives will go on for ever, that there could have been nothing of importance before we appeared on the scene. But it's not true. Life went on before our advent and will continue to do so after we are dead, so why strive to achieve the kind of material success we're talking about? Ultimately a man's life is judged on its quality. Has he had a happy life—a fulfilled existence? And surely people are the most important thing. And they cannot be bought—at least, the people who matter can't.'

Alexandra stared at him. 'That's a fascinating philosophy!' she exclaimed eagerly.

His expression was wry. 'Yes. Well, I guess that's what comes of living in a world where time has lost all meaning. Perhaps one day you'll understand what I mean. What was it Gray said? Something about many a flower being born to blush unseen ...'

'... and waste its sweetness on the desert air,' finished Alexandra, with a smile. 'Yes, I think I understand that now. But it's still a shame!'

The road was descending quite steeply now, and the undergrowth on each side gave an illusive sense of security which disappeared entirely when they emerged on the rim of a gorge below which a narrow torrent seethed and surged over ragged black rocks. Alexandra cast a horrified look in

Declan's direction, and he said:

'Don't be alarmed. We don't have to go down there. At least, not intentionally!'

'But aren't we nearly there?' she asked appealingly.

'Oh, yes,' he nodded. 'This place is called Ravina de Diablo—Devil's Ravine. You realised, of course, that Paradiablo means *to the devil*!'

'No. No, I didn't.' She shrugged. 'I didn't think about it.' She looked round. 'What a lonely place. Where is the village?'

'Across the gorge.' His mouth mocked her. 'Relax. It's not much further.'

Alexandra wished she could relax, but her earlier tension had returned and with it her nausea. How on earth were they to cross the gorge? There didn't appear to be any bridge. And in any case, who could build a bridge here, so many miles from civilisation? Her nails curled into her palms. And where was her father? And what kind of accommodation was she expected to occupy? She thought longingly of a bath and a change of clothes, such simple pleasures which now appeared the height of luxury. And somehow the prospect of sleeping again in a hammock filled her with despair.

She fought back the intense weariness which was threatening to overwhelm her. She was tired, that was all, she told herself, and it had been an exhausting day. She would feel entirely different after she had spoken with her father and had some sleep.

The station wagon was slowing perceptibly and a sharp bend in the track brought them to the very brink of the ravine. It was narrower at this point, two jutting wedges of rock providing a platform above the chasm, and connecting the two there was slung a rope walk, wide enough for a man to cross.

Alexandra turned to look at Declan in the fading light,

her lips parting in dismay. 'Do we—have we to cross that?' she asked in horror.

Declan brought the car to a halt beside a rough wooden building that stood like a sentinel beside the primitive bridge. 'I'm afraid so,' he agreed, switching off the engine. 'But I promise you the journey is over.'

Alexandra pushed open her door and climbed out, staring impotently across the gorge. In the fast invading gloom it was impossible to distinguish anything beyond a thick belt of trees that seemed to form a wall at the far end of the rope walk and there seemed no possible sign of a village at all.

Declan was unloading their gear and she had, perforce, to go round and help him. However, all he would permit her to carry was his haversack which he helped her to sling on her back, while he shouldered her cases and hand luggage.

'Come on,' he said, 'follow me. If you hold on to the sides you'll be all right. If you're nervous don't look down!'

Alexandra was nervous, but of course she had to look down, and her legs trembled violently. The bridge had been made out of plaited creepers worn smooth by the passage of time, and it swung and swayed above the chasm like a pendulum. Declan was obviously used to its unsteady motion and he measured his steps to its oscillating rhythm, progressing much more quickly than Alexandra. She moved slowly, clinging tightly to the ropes, terrified in case her earlier dizziness returned.

Halfway across she heard a dog begin barking, an eager excited sound that caused her brows to draw together uncomprehendingly. What was a dog doing here, apparently miles from anywhere? She didn't even know the villagers kept dogs.

Declan reached the opposite bank and turned to give her a hand to make the final leap from bridge to reassuringly solid rock. 'All right?' he enquired, and she nodded without enthusiasm.

But then she realised that what she had imagined was an impenetrable wall of trees was in fact a high wooden fence, and even as she absorbed this startling fact Declan was opening a gate in the fence and urging her forward.

The source of the barking was soon evident when two massive wolfhounds confronted them, growling suspiciously at Alexandra. She checked, her whole system freezing before their menacing attitudes, but at a word from Declan their hackles fell and they fussed about him, wagging their tails and licking his hands, and generally showing him how pleased they were to see him.

He closed the gate and Alexandra looked rather doubtfully about her. They were standing, amazingly, on a paved footpath that disappeared between hedges of flowering shrubs whose perfume was intoxicating on the night air. They could almost have been in a garden, she thought, were such a thing not ridiculous out here.

Declan gave her a wry smile before going ahead with the dogs and leaving her to follow him along the path. He had switched on his torch and she was glad of that small pool of light moving ahead of her. Darkness had fallen swiftly as it always did in the tropics and the coolness of the air was accentuated by their extra height above sea level.

She was so intent on looking down to see where she was going that she was not conscious of the lights ahead of her until they emerged into a clearing. And even then she was totally unprepared for the brooding beauty of the rambling, log-constructed house that confronted her. It was a one-storeyed dwelling, backed by trees, with a sloping roof and overhanging eaves that shaded a verandah. Shallow steps led up to a mesh door, while all the windows had shutters, bolted against the onslaught of moths and other flying insects attracted by the light. Tubs of clematis stood beside the posts that supported the eaves, and clustered in clumps between the woodwork. Light spilled through the mesh doorway and even as they approached an elderly woman wearing a long apron appeared at the top of the steps and came hurrying down to greet them. She was small and dark, a mixture of Indian and Portuguese, Alexandra guessed, and she spoke to Declan in that language until he interrupted her.

'English, Consuelo, *por favor*,' he enjoined quietly. 'This is Miss Tempest. She is to be our house guest. She is the daughter of Professor Tempest, you understand?'

As the little woman nodded and turned to her, Alexandra's startled brain registered what Declan had just said —that she was to be *his* house guest! She swallowed convulsively. What did he mean? Was this beautiful house his? And if so, was her father staying here?

It was hard to take it all in after the anxieties of the journey, and as though sensing this Declan put his hand beneath her elbow and urged her up the steps.

'You have prepared a room?' he was asking Consuelo, and she replied that she had, and that she would have a meal prepared in next to no time.

Alexandra looked helplessly up into Declan's face. 'My father . . .' she began, but he shook his head.

'Not yet,' he said, and his statement brooked no argument. 'Consuelo will show you to your room, you can bathe and change, and then we will discuss your father, right?'

Alexandra gave in. His words—the prospect of being able to wash the dirt of the journey from her body had become the most important thing, and she couldn't suppress a certain curiosity to see more of the house.

Inside the mesh door was an enormous living area. The unpolished log walls were a fitting backcloth to the huge brown leather couch and armchairs which flanked the wide stone fireplace. A log fire burned brightly in the grate, glinting on the ornamental shields and hunting spears that adorned the walls. There were skin rugs on the floor, and shelves of books filled the spaces beside the chimney breast. The lighting was provided by two hanging lamps of burnished copper that gleamed from hours of patient polishing. A low table before the hearth supported a solid-looking gold lighter, shaped like a small cannon, and an opened box of Havana cigars. There was a cupboard displaying an elaborate choice of spirits, and a bureau at which someone had obviously been working and had left a disarray of papers. At the opposite end of the room there was an eating area with dark wood chairs and a polished table where a bowl of exotic calla lilies provided a brilliantly vivid splash of colour.

Altogether it was one of the most attractive rooms Alexandra could ever remember seeing, and her brow furrowed as she followed Consuelo over to a heavy door which opened into a long hallway. She was conscious that Declan had followed them into the room and was presently helping himself from the cupboard containing the alcohol with the familiarity of long use. She shook her head. Who was he? This man who, because of his rapport with the Indians, she had assumed was an adventurer of some sort? And what was he doing living here in such state miles from people of his own kind?

Her thoughts were interrupted when Consuelo halted beside a closed door some distance along the hall. She indicated that Alexandra should wait outside for a moment and a few seconds later she had lit a lamp and was beckoning the girl to enter.

It was another attractive apartment, very much like the living room but without the shields and spears on the wall, and of course there was no fireplace. The furniture was huge and old-fashioned, but the wide bed looked wonderfully comfortable beneath its antique tapestry spread. A faint scent of beeswax mingled with the lingering smell of the spirit Consuelo had used to light the lamp, and to Alexandra, expecting to spend the night slung in a hammock beneath the thatched roof of a native hut, it looked like heaven.

'See!' Consuelo picked up the lamp after assuring herself that their guest had shown a fitting amount of enthusiasm about the sleeping arrangements. 'You wash in here.'

Alexandra followed her across to an inner door and allowed herself to be propelled into what appeared to be the bathroom. Consuelo held the lamp high and smiled her satisfaction at Alexandra's surprise at finding an enormous porcelain bath and basin, fed by a gas boiler, and a throne-like lavatory.

'Senhor O'Rourke make this for the guest,' said Consuelo, with evident pride. 'Your bathroom. No one else's.' She shook her head.

'It's—marvellous!' Alexandra made a helpless gesture. 'I don't know what to say.'

Consuelo seemed to find her reaction satisfactory, for she said: 'The *senhorita* would like a bath, eh? Consuelo will bring your bags and unpack them for you while you wash, yes?'

'Really, that's not necessary——' Alexandra began, feeling slightly dazed, but Consuelo had set down the lamp in the bedroom again and had disappeared out of the door.

Left alone, Alexandra moved across and closed the bedroom door and then looked about her. This whole affair was assuming the proportions of a rather extravagant dream and she found it hard to assimilate the events of the past twenty-four hours with any coherency. What was it Declan O'Rourke had said? That one could pass through all the seasons here in one day? She felt as if she had passed through the whole gamut of emotions during the past twenty-four hours.

A long mirror in the heavy wardrobe revealed her worst

fears. She looked an absolute mess! Her hair had not been brushed that morning, and hung in rats'-tails about her shoulders, her face was weary and streaked with dirt, her shirt and jeans looked as if she had slept in them, which in fact she had, and her hands were rough and grubby. What must her host have thought of her? In spite of the primitive conditions he had managed to appear clean and reasonably tidy, only the stubble on his chin bearing witness to his lack of shaving.

With an exclamation of disgust, she thrust off her boots and picking up the lamp marched into the bathroom. The plug was already in the bath, so she turned on the taps and watched the spray of hot water with real pleasure. Huge, soft bath sheets were folded neatly on a cork-topped stool and there was plenty of soap and sponges.

Without waiting for Consuelo to come back with her own things, Alexandra closed the door and stripped off her clothes eagerly. Climbing into the warm water was a pleasure to be savoured and she sank down luxuriously into the depths, uncaring that her hair was getting wet in the process. It was so good to feel the sweat seeping away from her and to relax completely without fear of intrusion.

Her new-found freedom from tension was shattered dramatically when the bathroom door opened and Consuelo came uninvited into the room. Alexandra jack-knifed into a sitting position, pressing a huge sponge protectively against her breast, but the old woman took no notice of her embarrassment.

'I have found your toothbrush, *senhorita*. I thought you would like to use it.' She smiled down at the girl. 'Is good, yes?'

'Yes, thank you.' Alexandra didn't know what to say.

Consuelo looked well pleased. 'Come,' she said. 'I will help you.'

Alexandra gasped. '*No*—really, it's all right——'

Consuelo ignored her, shaking her head in that knowing way as though assuming that Alexandra's protest was a mere formality. She reached for a sponge, soaped it liberally and began rubbing the girl's back.

'You will feel better after this, *senhorita*,' she said determinedly, pushing Alexandra's hair aside. 'Ay, ay, this hair is needing the wash, too.' Without warning, she scooped up a handful of water and soaked the crown of Alexandra's head. 'Come, Consuelo will wash hair and then she must go and get supper ready, yes?'

It was no good protesting, Alexandra had realised that. And in any case, it was quite pleasant feeling the old woman's hands massaging her scalp, rubbing at her hair until it was squeaky clean. Then she produced an elastic band, secured it on the top of Alexandra's head and left her to finish alone.

It was not until Alexandra began soaping her midriff that her fingers encountered the elastic plaster and a wave of remembered horror swept over her. She was glad Consuelo had not noticed that. She might have insisted on examining it for herself.

By the time she was ready to climb out, Alexandra felt infinitely better. The bath had removed some of the weariness from her limbs, and the knowledge that she could expect a good night's sleep for once had done wonders for her.

As she rubbed her hair with the towel, she wondered when she would see her father. She had the suspicion that he was not here at the moment, and she couldn't help but feel a sense of relief that she was going to have the opportunity to meet him on equal terms instead of dirty and dishevelled as she had been when she arrived. She had no doubt now that had he met her on her arrival he would have been absolutely furious.

Carrying the lamp back into the bedroom, a towel draped

57

sarong-wise about her body, she found that Consuelo had opened her cases but had only unpacked fresh underwear and a nightdress. Alexandra put the nightdress aside and opened up the other case, pulling out a cream caftan which she used about the house at home. It was a simple but expensive garment, long and straight with slits to knee level at either side and a low dipping neckline.

By the time she had smoothed a moisturising cream into her skin and stroked her lids with eyeshadow her hair was partially dry, sufficiently so to allow her to separate it into two bunches which she secured with thick hair-slides. She looked very young, she thought impatiently, but it couldn't be helped, and quite honestly she was feeling so hungry she didn't care much about her appearance right now.

Consuelo had told her to leave the lamp in the bedroom, so she turned it low before going out of the room and along the dimly lit hall to the living room. Delicious odours of food drifted along the passageway, and her earlier nausea disappeared completely.

When she entered the living room she thought at first that it was deserted, but as she turned to close the door a tall figure rose from his lounging position on the couch before the crackling fire. It was Declan O'Rourke, bathed and shaved, the water still glistening on his dark hair. He had changed, too, and was now wearing a dark red velvet jacket over close-fitting black suede pants, and although his white shirt was open at the neck it was evidently made of fine silk. He looked totally different from the casually indolent escort she had become used to, and it made the years between them so much more obvious somehow. She felt childish and unsophisticated in her simple gown, and the faintly mocking twist to his mouth did nothing for her confidence. He had a glass between his fingers and he raised it towards her in a sardonic salute before swallowing the remainder of its contents in a single gulp.

He looked down at the glass for a moment, before saying: 'Can I offer you an aperitif, Miss Tempest? Some fruit juice, perhaps—iced, of course.'

Alexandra moved across the room. 'I'd prefer a Martini, if it's not too much trouble,' she declared, refusing to be intimidated by the brooding quality of those pale blue eyes. 'Iced, of course!'

He shrugged and walked over to the cabinet containing the bottles and glasses. 'Sit down,' he directed over his shoulder. 'It can be very cold at night here.'

'I had noticed.' Alexandra was pleased with her rejoinder. It sounded right, just mildly sarcastic.

He poured her Martini, added ice, and brought it back to her. She had seated herself on the edge of one of the massive leather armchairs and she looked up at him coolly and thanked him politely. His eyebrows raised just a fraction and then he turned back to the cabinet and poured himself another drink. It looked like Scotch that he was taking, and she wondered how many he had had. Then he came to stand before the fire, his back to the flames.

'*Salud!*' he remarked, raising his glass, and she made a suitable response. 'Tell me,' he want on, 'Consuelo didn't scrub your back too hard, did she? She gets a little carried away at times.'

Alexandra's lips parted. 'How——' she was beginning, and then stopped herself. She had been about to fall into the trap he had set for her by stating something so disconcerting. Instead, she said: 'Do you speak from experience, Mr. O'Rourke?' in remarkably controlled tones.

He smiled, inclining his head in acknowledgement of her small victory. 'As a matter of fact, I do, Miss Tempest. Although, as I've known Consuelo since I was a very small boy, perhaps that excuses me somewhat.' He chuckled. 'Not that anything would deter Consuelo if she set her mind to it.'

Alexandra found her cheeks turning pink in spite of herself, and she sighed impatiently. 'Don't you think it's about time we started discussing the reason I'm here, Mr. O'Rourke?'

Declan considered the liquid in his glass. 'If you like.'

Alexandra waited for him to go on and when he didn't she gave an exasperated exclamation. 'Where is my father, Mr. O'Rourke?' she demanded. 'He's not here, is he?'

Declan hesitated. Then: 'No, I'm afraid not.'

Alexandra drew a deep breath. 'But he has been here?'

'Yes.'

'Then where is he? This was the only address he sent me!'

Declan swallowed some of his Scotch and looked down at her broodingly. 'As a matter of fact, your father is in hospital,' he said, slowly. 'In Bogota. I flew him there myself four days ago.'

CHAPTER FOUR

ALEXANDRA'S hand shook so much that she almost spilled her Martini into her lap. Declan reached down and removed the glass from her fingers, placing it on the stone mantelshelf beside him.

'I'm sorry,' he said quietly, 'but I thought it best not to burden you with it until we were here.'

Alexandra swallowed convulsively. 'But—but why have you brought me here? Why didn't you simply fly me to Bogota, too?'

Declan's mouth turned down at the corners. 'You'd have liked me to do that? In the state you were in?'

Alexandra hunched her shoulders, looking down at her hands. He was right, of course. She had not been fit to take anywhere, and certainly not to a hospital!

She looked up. 'You haven't told me why my father is in hospital. What's wrong? Is—is it serious?'

Declan finished his Scotch and stood his empty glass on the mantelshelf beside hers. 'That depends,' he said slowly.

'What do you mean?'

'Your father has contracted a certain kind of blood poisoning from the experiments he's been conducting.'

'Blood poisoning!' Alexandra moved her hands helplessly. 'I see.'

'Do you know anything about blood poisoning?'

Alexandra shrugged. 'A little. Do you?'

'A little, as you say,' he commented mildly.

'So how is he? Is he responding to treatment? When can

61

I see him?'

Declan thrust his hands into the pockets of his velvet jacket. 'Your father will no doubt recover in time. There is no need for alarm.'

'Then why is he still in hospital? You said you took him to Bogota four days ago.'

'So I did.' Declan nodded. 'However, septicaemia isn't always simple to diagnose, and the kind of work your father has been doing didn't help matters.'

'Septicaemia?'

'The medical term for blood poisoning.'

'Oh!'

'In septicaemia, an exact diagnosis of the bacteriological cause is essential. In your father's case, it was difficult at first to isolate the particular bacillus involved.'

Alexandra shook her head. 'Are there many types?'

'Several. The most virulent being the streptococcus organism which can enter the system through a mere scratch of which the victim may be totally unaware. Such was the case with your father, and that happens to be the type of poisoning he developed.'

Alexandra's throat felt dry. 'I see.' She felt a weak sense of relief that all was apparently to be well. What on earth would she have done if Declan O'Rourke had not appeared on the scene with her father hundreds of miles away in the hospital at Bogota? It was to be hoped that no message had been cabled to Aunt Liz or she would be terribly anxious about her. 'I—could I have my drink?' she asked jerkily, and after it was handed to her: 'I—I suppose I must thank you, for—for rescuing me and bringing me here.'

Declan gave her a fleeting look. 'Yes. Well, don't feel too obliged. I'd have done the same for anyone in the circumstances.'

'Perhaps. But nevertheless, I am grateful.' She finished the Martini. 'Do you—do you think I could have that fruit juice now? I am—very thirsty.'

With a brief inclination of his head he took her glass and turned away and as he did so the door opened and Consuelo came in wheeling a trolley. Alexandra now saw that the polished table at the end of the room had been set with raffia place mats and silver cutlery, and the old woman wheeled the trolley of food towards it and began putting out the dishes.

'You will please come and eat, *senhor*? *Senhorita*?' she asked, and Declan nodded.

'Indeed we will, Consuelo,' he affirmed lightly. 'I, for one, am starving!'

Although Alexandra's appetite had waned somewhat at the news about her father, the tantalising smell of curry brought her obediently to her feet and Consuelo indicated the chair she wished her to sit in. Declan brought the glass of iced lemon juice he had poured for her to the table and seated himself opposite, putting the glass within her reach.

The meal was absolutely delicious. Iced pineapple preceded the tangiest of curries, served on a bed of flaky rice, and for dessert there was a concoction of fruit and nuts that was very sticky and very sweet. Declan had a bottle of white wine with the meal, but Alexandra refused to take any of it, preferring the iced lemon juice he had given her. In consequence, he drank most of it himself, and she tried not to watch him refilling his glass. The coffee which Consuelo served on the low table before the fire afterwards was the finishing touch to the first real meal Alexandra had had since leaving Manaus, and she lay back in one of the leather armchairs feeling sleepily replete.

Declan occupied the couch, lighting a cigar and inhaling with evident enjoyment. He had poured himself a balloon-shaped glass of brandy to drink with his coffee, and cradling the glass between his fingers, he said: 'Don't hurry up in the morning. I shall be away for most of the day, and the

63

rest will do you good.'

His words had the effect of banishing her tiredness. 'You'll be away?' she echoed. 'Oh, but when will I see my father?'

Declan lounged back against the soft upholstery. 'That rather depends,' he remarked, savouring a mouthful of brandy. 'As he doesn't know you're here, I suggest we don't tell him. At least, for the time being.'

Alexandra sat up. 'Why not?'

'Your father is a sick man, Miss Tempest. Would you increase his anxieties by letting him know that you're here? Do you think that information will please him? Because I don't.'

She knew that, as usual, he was right. But she wouldn't give in that easily. 'I should have thought that seeing me might speed his recovery,' she said. 'After all, he must be feeling very isolated in Bogota, away from everyone he knows. I can book in at a hotel——'

'I shouldn't,' he interrupted coolly. 'Your father is not isolated at all. His research assistant from the laboratory in Rio is with him. Naturally, as she was involved, she felt a certain amount of responsibility, and as her family live in Bogota . . .'

'A woman assistant?' Alexandra felt blank.

'Yes. Juana de los Vargos. Didn't you know about her either?'

Alexandra pressed her lips tightly together. She hated the small smile that was tilting the corners of his firm mouth. She had never even heard of Juana de los Vargos, and he knew it. Why, she hadn't even known that her father had taken a research assistant with him.

'Even so——' she began defensively, but again he shook his head.

'Look, Alexandra——'

'I don't recall giving you permission to use my Christian

64

name!'

His smile deepened. 'Look, Alexandra,' he said again, 'I may not know your father as well as you think you do, but I'd hazard a guess that your appearance out here won't exactly endear you to him.'

'What do you mean? How dare you suggest——'

'I'm not suggesting anything. I'm telling you. Your place was in school——'

'School has finished for the summer holidays. And in any case, I shall be leaving school at Christmas——'

'Nevertheless, other arrangements had been made, hadn't they?'

'Yes,' she admitted reluctantly. 'I was to go to Cannes with my aunt.'

'There you are, then. Why didn't you go? Instead of coming trekking out here, putting yourself within reach of all manner of horrible diseases, tempting fate to set you down far more roughly than I am doing!'

Alexandra rose to her feet. 'I don't think any of this has anything to do with you, *Mr.* O'Rourke!'

He looked lazily up at her. 'Don't you?'

'No.' She coloured suddenly. 'Just because you're— you're providing me with accommodation for the night——'

'Oh, honey, it'll be much longer than one night!'

'What's that supposed to mean?'

'I have my work to do. I can't waste time taking you to Bogota for your father to send back again!' His lips twitched. 'That is, providing he doesn't order you straight back to England.'

Alexandra drew herself up to her full height, and endeavoured to appear composed. 'Then I shall find some other way of getting there. And until I do I'll find other lodgings—after tonight!'

'Do you mind telling me where?' His voice had hardened.

Alexandra shrugged. 'I imagine there are other white people about here, aren't there?'

'Two,' he agreed, nodding. 'The missionary and his wife at the village some distance down the track; but as their house has only one room beside the bedroom I hardly think they could accommodate you.'

Alexandra moved restlessly. 'I'll manage somehow.'

'No, you won't.' He rose to his feet now and although she was a tall girl he was still a great deal taller. 'You will stay here, as I have said, and if you attempt to disobey me I shall have no compunction about transporting you back to Rio myself! Is that clear?'

'I—I could come back——' she ventured.

'Yes, you could. But I somehow doubt that you would attempt such a journey again, having experienced it once.'

Her eyes were stormy. 'That's not fair!'

'No, it's not. But what you did wasn't entirely fair either, was it?'

'I love my father. I wanted to be with him——'

'—and you thought it would be a pretty adventure, didn't you? Something to brag about when you got back to school? Not the life and death survival it turned out to be!'

'I could fly back,' she retorted. 'I didn't know about that air-strip before.'

His eyes were cold and forbidding. 'The air-strip is private. It belongs to me.'

'Oh, well ...' she said defeatedly, but he wasn't finished.

'Make no mistake, Alexandra, I am a man of my word. Believe me, your father's wrath is nothing compared to mine.'

Alexandra lifted her slim shoulders. 'Have—have you sent word about my father to Aunt Elizabeth?'

'No.' He frowned. 'Should I have done?'

'Oh, no,' she breathed more freely. 'No. She would only

66

worry.'

He nodded. 'Right. Is that settled, then?'

'Do I have any choice?'

'Not a lot.'

'That's what I thought.' She shrugged. 'Do you have any objections if I go to bed now?'

Declan shook his head. 'Of course not. I'll be along in a few minutes to examine you.'

'Examine me?' A faint note of hysteria lifted her voice.

'Of course. The leech—remember?'

Alexandra's shoulders sagged. 'I'd forgotten.'

'I thought you had.' He moved to open the door for her. 'I'll see you later.'

She hesitated in the doorway. She was strangely loath to leave the comfort and security of the warm room. It had been a curiously unreal day, and the delayed shock of discovering that her father was in hospital was only now beginning to take effect. She felt totally alien in this alien place, and this man suddenly seemed her only link with the world she had known. She felt young and inexperienced and chokingly vulnerable.

As though sensing her highly emotional state he put a reassuring hand to the curve of her cheek. 'Relax,' he adjured gently. 'No one will hurt you here. And when your father comes back...'

Alexandra drew away. She didn't want his sympathy. She didn't trust herself not to break down under it and make a complete fool of herself. With a brief nod she walked quickly along the hall to her room, going inside and closing the door firmly behind her.

Then she leaned back against it, aware of a peculiar weakening in her legs. For a moment there she had been tempted to give in to tears, had *wanted* to do so, had wanted him to put his arms around her and draw her close against him. Her lips parted. She must be crazy thinking

67

thoughts like that! Just because last night ...

She moved determinedly away from the door and began to unbutton the caftan. She was allowing her natural anxiety about her father to colour her reason. She had always been brought up to be independent, to look after herself. She had never had anyone to mentally pick her up in times of trouble. Aunt Liz had always been in the background, of course, but she was a spinster lady who had grown accustomed to hiding her feelings. Her brother, Alexandra's father, had frowned upon demonstrations of what he termed 'lack of control', and Alexandra had learned to hide her tears and always put on a brave face in her father's presence. Which all made this weakness she was feeling now even more incomprehensible.

The nightdress Consuelo had unpacked earlier was laid out on the bed and while she had been having dinner the rest of her things had been unpacked for her. She shook her head helplessly. What to wear, that was the problem. She could hardly put on a nightdress when he expected to look at her midriff!

She eventually decided to remain dressed, but in suitable garments, and an inspection of the drawers of the chest produced a cotton blouse which conveniently left her midriff bare. There didn't appear to be any reddening of the flesh around the plaster, she decided thankfully, as she buttoned the waistband of a pair of blue cotton trousers, and when, a few moments later, there was a knock at her door, she went to answer it with the intention of dismissing his attentions.

'Going somewhere?' he greeted her dryly, looking down at the blouse and trousers.

'No,' She ignored the way he could embarrass her at will. 'But there's no need for you to examine me. It looks perfectly all right now, thank you.'

Declan propelled the door open without apparent effort.

'Really?' He entered her room uninvited. 'I'll decide what does and what does not require my attention, if you don't mind? Or do you want to end up in hospital, too?'

Alexandra sighed. 'I don't think that's likely,' she exclaimed.

'Let us hope not.' He glanced round. 'I suggest you lie on the bed. It won't take a minute.'

Alexandra was about to protest again, but with a look at his unyielding countenance she acquiesced. 'Oh, well, if you insist . . .' she muttered, with ill grace, and obediently sat down on the soft springing mattress.

His expression enigmatic, he indicated that she should lie back, and then he knelt on one knee and swiftly removed the plaster. Alexandra winced as it clung to her skin, but then his probing fingers were moving against her flesh and other, more disruptive, sensations replaced her frustration. His hands were firm and cool, and as he bent his head to examine the puncture minutely she could smell the faint aroma of his after-shaving lotion. His hair fell thick and smooth against his forehead, apparently requiring no hair-dressing, and she had the most disturbing urge to touch it.

'Hmm,' he murmured at last. 'I don't think you're going to have any trouble with that if you do as you're told.'

He brought a packet containing a wedge of cotton wool and a tube of ointment out of his pocket and smeared the ointment liberally over the area. Then he produced another wider plaster from his other pocket and sealed it in position.

'All right,' he said, straightening. Alexandra sat up. 'I'll keep an eye on it. But for God's sake, if you scratch yourself while you're here, tell me!'

Alexandra nodded, summoning her resentment at his air of command over her to dispel the awareness of herself that he inspired in her.

He stood for a moment just looking down at her, and then he said impatiently: 'What is it? Why didn't you want me to touch you?'

Alexandra stiffened. 'I don't know what you mean——'

'Yes, you do.'

'I didn't say that ...'

'Not in so many words perhaps, but that was what you meant. And this elaborate display of modesty—what's it all for? Don't you suppose I have a memory?'

Alexandra's cheeks burned. 'Don't be crude!'

'Why not? It's what you appear to expect. What kind of society have you been moving in, Miss Tempest?' He shook his head mockingly.

Alexandra got to her feet, hating his cynicism. 'I'm tired, Mr. O'Rourke. Will you please leave my room?'

He looked down at the ointment-smeared cotton wool in his hands. 'Of course.' His smile was not pleasant. 'Forgive the intrusion.'

And with that he left her, closing the door behind him with a definite click.

Alexandra moved after him as though putting her weight against the door would dispel his lingering mockery. She felt she had never disliked anyone as she disliked him, and the tears which she had tried so hard to suppress refused to be denied any longer.

CHAPTER FIVE

ALEXANDRA spent the first half of the night fighting her way through hordes of imaginary tarantulas and plunging down the mountainside from the silver streak of the aircraft in which Declan had flown her to Paradiablo. She was unaccustomed to the confinement of the bedcovers and not until she had freed her legs and discarded her pillow did she fall into a deep slumber.

She awakened reluctantly to find sunlight streaming through the slats in her shutters. She lay for several minutes absorbing her surroundings and enjoying the sensation of waking without the recently familiar crick in her back, and then remembering what Declan had said about being away all day she reached for her watch.

She saw, to her astonishment, that it was after eleven, and she flopped back on the mattress, realising that he would be long gone. The knowledge aroused a sense of unwilling disappointment inside her and rather than acknowledge such an unpleasing revelation she thrust her legs over the side of the bed and encountered the cool wooden tiles of the floor.

She padded across to the windows taking care to look for any unwelcome visitors, but apart from a wall lizard which scuttled away at her approach the room was thankfully uninvaded. She unfastened the shutters with their meshed lining and thrust them open taking her first real look at the fantastic garden. It was just as she remembered it from the night before, a confusion of exotic shrubs and flowering

71

trees, the scents mingling in the heat to produce an intoxicating fragrance.

She was suddenly eager to be dressed and out in the day. She walked quickly to the bathroom, thrust open the door, and then halted, aghast, at the sight of half a dozen enormous black beetles crawling round the bath. She stepped backward and closed the door, shuddering uncontrollably.

'Ugh!' she moaned, feeling almost sick. Where on earth had they come from?

She stood for a moment, undecided what to do, and then rushed across to pull open the hall door and call: '*Consuelo!*'

Her voice sounded quavery even to her ears and she stamped her foot irritably. Good heavens, what was she? A woman, or a mouse? Or simply a rather silly girl?

'Consuelo?' she called again, more firmly this time, but the little woman did not appear.

'*Damn!*' Alexandra hesitated in the doorway. 'Oh, damn, damn, damn!'

A sudden draught of air behind her caused her to turn in alarm; but it was not Declan entering the house through the door at the end of the passage but a woman, in her late twenties, Alexandra guessed, with curling auburn hair and vividly attractive features.

'Such temper!' she observed, by way of a greeting, her hazel eyes assessing Alexandra very thoroughly. 'What's wrong? Have you lost something?'

Alexandra was intensely conscious of the scarcity of attire afforded by a pink cotton nightdress when compared to well-fitting cream slacks and a scarlet shirt which should have clashed with the woman's hair but somehow didn't.

However, Alexandra had been taught to be unfailingly polite, and as she recalled that Declan had told her that the missionary and his wife were the only other white people in the district, this woman had, amazingly, to be the missionary's wife. So she crossed her arms rather protectively across her breasts, and said: 'How do you do? No, I haven't lost anything. On the contrary, I think I've found something.'

The woman raised dark eyebrows. 'Really? What?'

Alexandra sighed, wishing Consuelo would appear and rescue her from this awkward situation. But she didn't, and Alexandra was forced to say: 'Actually, there are several beetles in the bath.'

The woman nodded knowingly. 'Oh, I see. I suppose you didn't replace the plug after using it.'

'Why no, I—I didn't.'

'I thought as much. They crawl up the waste pipe. You'll have to remember in future.' She frowned. 'I'm surprised they got up so quickly, though.' '

Alexandra looked blank. 'Quickly?'

'Well, if you've just had a bath——'

'No. I had it last night.'

'Oh! You're just getting up, then.' The woman made it sound like the height of self-indulgence.

'As a matter of fact, yes.' Alexandra was beginning to think she was going to get no help here. 'If you'll excuse me, I'll—I'll go and deal with them.'

'Would you like me to do it?' the woman offered. 'You were shouting Consuelo for that purpose, weren't you?'

Alexandra wondered if she appeared so transparent to everybody. After Declan O'Rourke's behaviour, and now this . . . She shrugged a little ungraciously. 'If you like.'

The woman gave a faint smile and brushed past her, crossing the bedroom with loose easy strides. One look encompassed the ugly intruders in the bath and quite callously she took off her shoe and massacred them all. Then she ran water into the bath, rinsed the mess away, and turned back to Alexandra.

'There you are. I should have Consuelo disinfect it before you use it again. I've put in the plug, as you can see.'

Alexandra tried to feel grateful, but there was something about the woman's attitude that jarred. She didn't know what it was, whether it was her air of command, or the way she walked unannounced into Declan's house, or simply the way her eyes appraised the younger girl and clearly found her wanting.

'Thank you,' she managed, accompanying the woman to the door. 'Er—I'm Alexandra Tempest. You must be the missionary's wife.'

'I'm Clare Forman, yes, and I know who you are. Declan told us all about you. He called this morning on his way out and asked me to come up and see that you weren't running into difficulties.'

Her patronising air was more pronounced than ever and Alexandra was tempted to tell her that she was perfectly all right, that she needed no one to watch out for her, and that she was going back to bed!

But of course, it wasn't her nature to be downright rude even though she now bitterly regretted letting Clare Forman get rid of the beetles. She would be able to tell Declan that within a couple of hours of his departure, she had been literally shouting for help!

'It was very kind of you to take the trouble, Mrs. Forman,' she got out through tight lips. 'But now I really must get dressed.'

'Yes. That would be a good idea.' Clare flicked a speck of dirt from the immaculate creases in her slacks. 'I'll go and rout Consuelo, and when you're ready we can have coffee together.'

Without giving Alexandra any time to protest, she walked away down the hall and the girl turned and went back into her bedroom, slamming the door with frustrated irritation behind her. She didn't want to have coffee with Clare Forman, but there was nothing she could do to prevent her from staying.

By the time she had washed and dressed in brief denim shorts and the cotton blouse she had put on for Declan's examination the night before, she was feeling a little better. Her skin was naturally a honey colour and she thought with satisfaction that several days of this heat would tan her a golden brown.

When she entered the living room a few minutes later, she found the mesh door to the verandah open, and Clare Forman talking to Consuelo outside. However, when the little housekeeper saw Alexandra she left the other woman and came hurrying through to greet her.

'The *senhorita* is looking much better this morning,' she said with satisfaction, viewing the brief shorts with a little giggle. 'Ay, ay, is this what they are wearing in London?'

Alexandra could not take offence at her interest. 'Do you like them?' she asked, doing a quick turnabout. 'I've got some orange ones which would suit you beautifully!'

Consuelo clasped her hands together mirthfully. 'Me? In such things?' She burst into blissful laughter, and for a moment they shared the joke. Then she sobered and said: 'The Senhora Forman is here. You have met her, yes?'

'Yes.' Alexandra caught her lower lip between her teeth. 'There were some beetles in the bath.'

'*Sim*, the *senhora* say so,' Consuelo nodded. 'Consuelo was outside when you call. I did not hear you.'

'It doesn't matter, really.' Alexandra gave a rueful glance towards the verandah.

'I get coffee,' said Consuelo, patting her arm. 'And perhaps you would like *os paozinhos*?'

'*Os paozinhos*?' Alexandra struggled to remember what few words of Portuguese she knew.

'She means rolls, *croissants*,' stated Clare Forman from the doorway. 'Yes, Consuelo, I'm sure Miss Tempest is hungry.'

75

Alexandra was, but rather than allow Clare Forman another victory, she said: 'Thank you, Consuelo, but coffee is all I need.'

Clare Forman shrugged and turned back to the chair she had been occupying on the verandah, while Alexandra smiled conspiratorially at Consuelo before going to join her.

It was very pleasant in the shade of the verandah. Beyond the courtyard the garden was a constant source of interest with huge butterflies with the wing-span of a man's hand and patterned in the most gorgeous colours vying with their feathered neighbours in brilliance. There were red-headed blackbirds, a species Santos had pointed out to her at Los ermanos, kingfishers the size of wood pigeons, and tiny humming birds whose wings beat so rapidly they actually sang. Alexandra was entranced. Everything was so much larger than life somehow, and she would have been quite content just to relax and watch what happened.

But once Consuelo had served the coffee, Clare was disposed to talk, and Alexandra had no choice but to answer her.

'Tell me,' she said, adding two spoonfuls of sugar to her brimming cup, 'whatever possessed you to come out here without warning anyone of your plans?'

Alexandra rested her elbows on the circular bamboo table. 'I wanted to surprise my father,' she replied simply.

'You'll do that without a doubt,' remarked Clare, her tone dry.

'Perhaps I will.' Alexandra resented the other woman's attitude. 'However, my reasons for being here are pretty obvious. How about yours?'

Clare was taken aback. 'Mine?'

'Yes. What brought your husband to a place like Paradiablo?'

Clare hesitated. Then she said slowly: 'My husband is the stuff of which pioneers are made. He sees his work here

76

as a challenge. Naturally, I accompanied him.'

'And have you been here long?'

'Eighteen months.'

'Quite a long time.' Alexandra made an involuntary gesture. 'What do you find to do?'

Clare shrugged, clearly not altogether happy with this line of questioning. 'I manage,' she replied shortly. 'And of course, Declan has made things so much easier for me.'

'Declan?' Alexandra looked puzzled and Clare gave a slow secretive smile.

'Yes. He makes me—and my husband—welcome here at any time. The conditions where we live are so—primitive! This house is civilisation!'

She stretched her arms encompassingly and Alexandra felt a slight stirring of distaste. Yes, she thought. Clare had entered the house as though sure of her welcome. And how often did she come here without her husband?

Pushing such disruptive thoughts aside, Alexandra reached for the coffee jug and refilled her cup. 'Mr. O'Rourke lives here then?' she asked casually.

Clare frowned. 'Of course. Why do you ask?'

Alexandra lifted her cup to her lips. 'It just seems—an odd place for anyone to build a house.'

Clare lay back in her chair. 'I see. You don't know anything about him, do you?'

Alexandra flushed. 'I wasn't particularly interested.'

'Weren't you? Not even when you were obliged to accept his hospitality?'

'I had no choice.'

'Agreed. But if Declan hadn't heard you were at Los Hermanos and gone to fetch you, you'd have been in deep trouble.' She studied the girl opposite appraisingly. 'Anyway, Declan didn't build this house. His father did.'

Alexandra acknowledged this with a brief inclination of her head, determined not to appear curious, but apparently

Clare was prepared to go on.

'His grandfather came here long before the river was opened up to Europeans. Lots of men did. The area has always attracted prospectors.'

'You mean—*gold* prospectors?' Alexandra couldn't prevent the question.

'Gold, silver—and most important of all, so far as Declan's grandfather was concerned, diamonds!'

'Diamonds!'

'Yes. Mostly industrial diamonds. When Patrick O'Rourke came here to Paradiablo, that stream down in the gorge was running with them.'

'You're not serious!'

'Oh, I am,' Clare shrugged. 'I've told you—it was a prospector's paradise. The only problem was the Indians. I'm sure you've read some of the gory stories brought back by unsuccessful explorers— headhunters, cannibalism, that sort of thing.'

Alexandra shivered. 'Who hasn't?'

'Indeed,' Clare nodded. 'Well, Declan's grandfather had the sure solution—he married the chief's daughter.'

Alexandra stared at her. 'You mean—Declan's grandmother was—an Indian?'

'That's right.' Clare laughed mockingly. 'Haven't you run up against that ruthless trait in him yet?' She poured herself some more coffee. 'Of course, it's been watered down—the Indian blood, I mean. Tom O'Rourke, Declan's father, was much more particular. He is a handsome devil, too. He married the daughter of a Portuguese banker in São Paulo and added considerably to the family fortune. Declan is their only son. It was Tom who built this house, but he's never lived in it. He used to use it as a sort of—retreat.' Her lips curved sensually. 'Perhaps he isn't as immune from his Indian ancestry as he would like to believe.'

Alexandra pushed her cup aside. She very much disliked

Clare's insinuative way of speaking. As if *she* were personally involved.

'Of course, Declan's been somewhat of a disappointment to them,' she went on thoughtfully. 'His father had a career in banking mapped out for him, but Declan chose to return to the country of his forebears. Perhaps that savage pride skipped a generation to emerge in him. Whatever the reasons, he feels a strong sense of identification with these people, and works to that end.'

'Works?' Alexandra frowned. 'You mean, he's still prospecting?'

'Prospecting? *Prospecting?* Oh, my God!' Clare burst out laughing. 'Prospecting? Oh, that's beautiful!' She shook her head helplessly. Then she sobered sufficiently to say: 'No, my dear. Not prospecting. Didn't he tell you? He's a doctor!'

'A *doctor*?' Alexandra was aghast. 'A—a real doctor?'

'Well, he's not a witch doctor, if that's what you mean,' gurgled Clare, enjoying the girl's confusion. 'Honestly, my dear, I assumed you knew *that*!'

Alexandra slid off her chair and walked to the edge of the verandah, resting her hands on the wooden rail. He was a doctor—and she felt ridiculously small. No wonder he had been so impatient with her. Did he think she knew? She gripped the rail very tightly. She *should* have known, she should have guessed from his manner, from his knowledge of her father's illness—a hundred and one small clues were suddenly staring her in the face.

She moved her shoulders defensively. Well, she hadn't known. But now that she did, she ought to apologise ...

She heard a movement behind her and turned to find Clare lighting a cigarette. Inhaling deeply, she said: 'What's that plaster on your midriff? Has Declan been treating you already?'

Alexandra bent her head, her fingers moving automatic-

79

ally to cover the dressing. 'Oh—well, yes. But it's nothing really. A—a leech attached itself to me in the night.'

Clare grimaced. 'Ghastly things, aren't they? I once heard of a man collapsing with fever in the jungle, and when they eventually found him he was covered in the things, and hadn't a drop of blood left in his body——'

'Thank you, Clare, that will do!'

Declan's deep tones startled both of them. He was standing in the open doorway of the house, lean and handsome in a denim battle jacket over close-fitting denim pants which were thrust into knee-length black boots. He wore no shirt and his chest was damp with sweat.

Alexandra had to drag her eyes away from him. There was something so physically attractive about him that she was almost glad of Clare's presence to distract his attention while she sought for composure. He thrust his hands into the pockets of his trousers, tautening the cloth across his thighs, and a small smile played about his mouth as he noted the brief shorts and blouse.

Then Clare rose elegantly to her feet and interceded. 'Now, darling,' she murmured, 'I was only telling Miss Tempest a little about the real dangers of the Amazon. Surely you have no objections.' She moved a little closer, looking up at him appealingly. 'Besides, you told me you were to be away all day!'

'I intended to be.' Declan stretched lazily. 'But I decided it was too much to expect Alexandra to spend the whole of her first day here alone.'

'Alone?' Clare raised her eyebrows. 'That's hardly flattering. I'm here.'

'I wasn't to know that.'

'You asked me to come.' Clare was charmingly petulant.

'I asked you to call and make sure Alexandra was all right. I didn't think you'd stay.'

Clare glanced mockingly towards Alexandra. 'Oh, Alex

and I have been getting on like a house on fire, haven't we, Alex?'

Alexandra shrugged. She hated the diminutive use of her name, and what Clare really meant was that she had been enjoying herself immensely by making a fool of her. But she could hardly say that to Declan, so she made some mumbled assent and was conscious that his gaze lingered on her rather longer than was necessary.

'Anyway, it's lunchtime,' announced Clare, glancing at her watch. 'Am I invited to stay?'

Declan made a slight bow. 'Of course, if you would like to do so.'

'I should.' Clare smiled contentedly. 'David's gone to Timbale and won't be home until this evening, so I'm quite free.'

Alexandra scuffed her toe against the roughened planks of the verandah floor. If Clare was staying she would have no opportunity to speak to Declan alone and explain that she had been unaware of his status and apologise. And it was quite on the cards that Clare would find some way to ridicule her in front of him. Quite suddenly, she wanted to leave, to get away from them. It was stupid, Clare was the missionary's wife, after all, but somehow her attitude towards Declan had a certain possessive intimacy about it, and Alexandra felt sickened by it.

However, Declan excused himself at that moment, saying that he needed to bathe and change his clothes before the meal. Clare reseated herself, evidently pleased with the way things were going, and Alexandra took the opportunity to gather together the coffee cups on to a tray and say that she was just taking them through for Consuelo. She had no real idea where the kitchen was, but there were not too many doors opening off the hall that she found it any difficulty. The little Portuguese woman smiled her thanks.

'Senhora Forman is staying for lunch,' she said, tighten-

81

ing her lips. 'That woman!' She shook her head.

Alexandra would have liked to have lingered to gossip, but she knew that such a thing was not advisable. So she made some deprecatory rejoinder and left the room.

In the hall, an idea struck her. Declan was alone at the moment. Now was her opportunity to explain. Probably the only opportunity she would have that day.

She looked round. A heavy door stood slightly ajar and with trembling fingers she propelled it far enough open to see into the room beyond. It was Declan's room, she saw that instantly. His discarded denim suit was lying untidily on the bed, and there was the sound of water running in an adjoining bathroom.

Glancing over her shoulder to assure herself that Clare was nowhere about, Alexandra advanced into the room, closing the door behind her and leaning back against it. She was surprised to find that the palms of her hands were suddenly moist, and that curious weakness was invading her legs again.

An awful awareness of exactly what she was doing splintered her resolve. What would her father think if he could see her hiding in this man's bedroom? What would Clare Forman think if she suddenly decided to come looking for her?

With a dry throat, she moved a little away from the door preparatory to opening it, concentrating on turning the handle without making the least sound. Then hard fingers were biting into her shoulder and Declan's voice near her ear was saying: 'What the hell do you think you're doing?'

Alexandra released the handle and swung round to lean back weakly against the door. Declan was hitching a towel, his only covering, about his lean hips, and was regarding her with impatient blue eyes. 'I—I—this is the wrong room——' she faltered.

'Is it?'

82

His hair was wet and shiny and clung to his neck. Alexandra's breathing became hopelessly uneven. 'I—I did want to speak to you, but then—I changed my mind.'

'Why?'

She made an involuntary movement of her shoulders. 'I shouldn't have come in here.'

His expression was wry. 'That rather depends what you have to say.'

Alexandra took a deep breath. 'Mrs. Forman told me you were a doctor!'

Declan raked his hair back from his forehead. 'Oh, I see.'

'I didn't know. You didn't tell me, and—well, how could I?'

'Have I said you should?'

'No, but...' Alexandra's voice trailed away. 'I just wanted to say I was—sorry.'

'For what?' His eyes challenged hers.

'Oh, you know for what! For being rude—for—well, for behaving in that silly way last night.'

Declan's mouth twisted. 'I see.'

'You do believe me, don't you?'

'What else did—*Mrs.* Forman tell you?'

Alexandra felt the hot colour staining her cheeks. 'This and that.'

'In other words, you've been discussing me pretty thoroughly this morning.'

'*No!*' Alexandra was indignant. 'I—Mrs. Forman was just telling me about—about the diamonds.'

'And the fact that my grandmother was an Indian, no doubt,' he remarked laconically.

'Well—yes, that did come into it.'

'I thought it might.'

'Well, why not? It—it's nothing to be ashamed of.'

'Goddamn you, I know that!' His eyes were granite-hard. 'But do you?'

She moved uncomfortably. 'It's nothing to do with me.'

'Right.'

'But it wasn't me who was discussing it, was it? It—it was your friend Mrs. Forman.'

His eyes glinted. 'Exactly what is that supposed to mean?'

Alexandra swallowed with difficulty. 'W—what?'

'The accent upon *your friend*?'

'Well, she is your friend, isn't she?' retorted Alexandra, trying not to feel intimidated. 'She's certainly not mine.'

'Oh, no?'

'No.' She straightened. 'If you'll excuse me——'

'In a moment.' His hands were suddenly supporting his body pressed against the door somewhere near her ears, successfully imprisoning her. He was much nearer now, and she could see the pores of his brown skin, feel the warmth of his breath. 'What has Mrs. Forman said to make you assume that she and I are friends?'

Alexandra moved her head helplessly from side to side. 'Why, nothing.' She made a dismissing gesture. 'She didn't have to *say* anything.'

'Why not?'

His eyes narrowed. The long lashes were tipped with gold like the hair on his chest, and a curious pain stirred in the pit of her stomach. Although she had known this man such a comparatively short space of time their relationship had been artificially intensified by the circumstances they had shared and in consequence it had developed with the speed of everything else here. Her tongue came out to wet her lips. She was experiencing an intense desire to reach out and touch his damp skin, but she sensed that if she did so the whole situation could get rapidly out of hand. Her eyes lifted to his and for a moment she glimpsed a similar awareness there. But then he thrust himself away from her and strode swiftly across the room to disappear into the bathroom.

Alexandra's breathing was ragged. What had happened? Why had he walked away like that? Had she mistaken anger for provocation?

She stood, trying to think coherently, but when he eventually emerged again dressed in cream shirt and pants she was no nearer to a logical assimilation of what had occurred. He seemed annoyed to find that she was still there and his tone was curt as he said:

'You can go. I guarantee Mrs. Forman won't say anything to upset you now that I'm here.'

Alexandra felt humiliated. She turned quickly aside, reaching for the door handle, but again he stopped her, moving lithely to her side and allowing his fingers to close round the flesh of her upper arm.

'You're too sensitive!' he exclaimed impatiently. 'For God's sake, Alexandra, I realise you're just beginning to be aware of yourself as a female, but don't try that kind of experimentation on me!'

'I don't know what you mean!'

'Don't you?' He swung her round to face him. 'I think you do. I think you're ripe for some kind of sexual experience, but not with me!'

'How—how dare you?'

Alexandra was affronted. That he should imagine she had calculated what had happened! She would have liked to have slapped his sardonic face had he not looked so grim. As it was, she was too inexperienced to dare such reckless behaviour.

'Look——' he heaved a deep sigh. 'All right. This situation is an unnatural one, I'll grant you that. You didn't expect to have to stay here, and I sure as hell didn't want to bring you. But there seemed no alternative, short of despatching you back to England. Now I can do that if you'd

85

like me to, but somehow I don't think you do.'

Alexandra shook her head mutinously and he went on: 'So—we're here, and as we do have to spend some time together, I suggest we get a few things straight. I am not a sex-starved prospector, eager for the sight of a white woman! Nor do I get involved with infatuated teenagers, white or otherwise—do I make myself clear?'

Alexandra's cheeks burned, and he continued: 'But if some tremulous female creature comes uninvited into my bedroom and finds me practically stark naked and then accuses me of being involved in a not very reputable way with another woman, she is inviting the kind of retribution repayable in kind!'

'I—I didn't accuse you.'

'Not in so many words, perhaps, but the implication was there.'

'May I go now?' Alexandra was sulky.

Declan released her arm, and she looked down at the white marks the hard pressure of his fingers had made. 'Yes,' he said. 'You can go. If you like, I'll invite Mrs. Forman to stay while you're here. She would make a very adequate chaperon!'

Alexandra's lips parted in dismay. 'You—wouldn't!'

'Why not?'

Alexandra stared at him impotently for a moment longer and then she wrenched open the door and left the room, trembling as the heavy barrier banged behind her.

CHAPTER SIX

ALEXANDRA would have liked to have missed lunch, but as
she had not had any breakfast her stomach was beginning to
protest. So she sponged her hot cheeks with cool water in
her bathroom and returned to the living room just as Consuelo was wheeling in the food trolley.

There was a fish stew, served with wedges of the starchy
bread Alexandra was growing accustomed to, and fresh
fruit to follow. Coffee was served at the table, and the
younger girl sensed Consuelo's displeasure when Clare insisted that she placed the coffee pot and cups beside her so
that she could serve it herself. It was clear that the old
housekeeper liked the missionary's wife no more than did
Alexandra.

It had been a mainly silent meal, with Clare doing most
of what talking there was. Declan himself seemed absorbed
and thoughtful, answering only when spoken to and then
only in monosyllables.

Towards the end of the meal, Clare said: 'Well, really,
darling, I shouldn't have stayed if I'd known it was going to
be such a grim occasion. What is it? Are you beginning to
feel the weight of your responsibilities?'

Her glance flickered towards Alexandra, and the girl
moved uncomfortably. The memory of that scene in Declan's bedroom was still very clear in her mind and Clare's
words were a little too accurate for comfort.

Declan looked up from his contemplation of a wine glass.
'Perhaps I am,' he conceded, his eyes holding Clare's.

'What would you suggest I do about it?'

Clare visibly warmed to his attention. 'Well, my dear, there is only one thing to do, isn't there? Shed them!'

'How do I do that?' Declan was very still, his voice disturbingly quiet.

Clare shrugged. 'I should have thought that was obvious. Surely there must be some suitable ménage in Bogota——'

Alexandra was shocked out of her inertia. 'I already suggested that!' she burst out hotly, angry that Clare should dare to discuss her as if she wasn't present.

Declan looked at her resignedly. 'Cool down,' he advised. 'Clare is only baiting you.'

Clare lay back in her chair. 'Am I?'

'Well? Aren't you?'

She shrugged. 'Oh, I suppose so.' She sounded impatient, too. 'Even so, Alex can't go on living here with you—alone.'

'Why not?'

'I don't think her father would approve.'

'Her father's not here.'

'That's beside the point.'

'I disagree. Her father can hardly protest about something of which he knows nothing.'

'You intend keeping Alex's presence a secret?'

Declan's mouth turned down at the corners. 'Stop anticipating me. There's no secret involved. Professor Tempest will merely remain in ignorance of his daughter's arrival until he is fit enough to leave the hospital.'

Now it was Alexandra's turn to protest. 'You mean I'm not to see him until he comes back here?'

'I thought I had made the position plain to you.' Declan's eyes were hard as they rested on her. 'Your father is a sick man. I do not intend to do anything that might weaken his constitution, and knowing his only offspring has been foolish enough to venture alone into the Amazonian jungle is enough to cause him unnecessary anxiety. Anxiety causes stress, stress weakens——'

'Oh, all right.' Alexandra pushed back her chair and got to her feet. 'If you'll excuse me, I'll go to my room.'

Declan rose politely and inclined his head. 'I expect you're tired.'

'Yes.' Alexandra sounded doubtful, but her eyes shifted reluctantly to Clare's satisfied face. 'Goodbye, Mrs. Forman.'

'Cheerio, Alex. I expect we'll be seeing more of one another during the next few days. I hope your father doesn't take too long to recover.'

Alexandra forced a smile and then walked jerkily across the room, only relaxing when the door of her bedroom had closed behind her.

Alexandra spent the rest of the afternoon in her room. She was more tired than she had thought and she fell asleep almost at once, not waking until the sun was sinking rapidly and the cool shadows of evening were stealing across the bed. She washed in the bathroom, unable to look into the bath which Consuelo had scoured without feeling a twinge of remembered horror. Then she changed into a plain yellow cotton dress and walked along to the living room.

There was no sign of anybody and she stood hesitatingly in the middle of the floor, looking towards the darkening garden outside. It was strange how the tropical foliage had a totally unreal appearance in the half light, the colours muted, the birds uncannily silent, an eerie, lifeless landscape.

A sound behind her brought her round with a start, but she relaxed weakly when she saw Consuelo.

'Senhor O'Rourke has gone out, *senhorita*,' said the old housekeeper, going across to secure the mesh door and light the lamps. 'I expect he will be back later.'

Alexandra gathered herself. 'Gone out? Where has he gone?'

Consuelo adjusted the wick of the lamp and straightened. 'A child is sick, *senhorita*. He has gone to make it well.'

'Oh, I see.' Alexandra nodded. 'I—has Senhora Forman left, too?'

'*Sim, senhorita*.' Consuelo sounded very definite about that.

Alexandra was temped to ask her why she didn't appear to have much liking for the other woman, but a sense of disgust at her own duplicity kept her silent. Instead she rubbed her arms with the palms of her hands and said: 'It's much cooler now, isn't it?'

Consuelo nodded. 'Is always cooler in the mountains, *senhorita*. I will light the fire.'

Alexandra watched as Consuelo applied a match to the tinder-dry sticks already piled on the hearth. The wood crackled and flamed, and in the warming glow Alexandra felt the lingering traces of unease and isolation disappear. The garden no longer appeared a strange and alien barrier between herself and the outside world, but a secure and comforting setting for this beautiful house.

When Consuelo was satisfied that the logs she had put on top of the sticks would burn she turned back to her guest.

'You are hungry, *senhorita*? I will bring some food.'

Alexandra hesitated. 'Oh—well, if it's not too much trouble. I mean, shouldn't I wait for—for Mr. O'Rourke?'

'The *senhor* may not be back until late, *senhorita*. Consuelo will prepare supper.'

'Then can I help you?' Alexandra spread her hands. It was hard to explain, but right now she didn't want to be alone.

Consuelo frowned, but then she said: 'You wish to talk, *senhorita*? Come to the kitchen. Consuelo will prepare supper and we will talk, *sim*?'

Alexandra was not altogether convinced of he advisability of such a course, but she could not be rude and refuse, so she merely smiled and nodded, and said she would be interested to see the kitchen.

It was remarkably modern, with fitted units and a gas-operated oven and refrigerator. Consuelo was clearly very proud to be the owner of such a kitchen and she showed Alexandra how everything worked with a touching eagerness.

Something was cooking on the stove, but when Alexandra tentatively lifted the lid of the saucepan, she drew back from the concoction inside with scarcely concealed dismay. It appeared to be a stew of meat and vegetables and although it smelled appetising it looked revolting.

Consuelo, however, nodded happily. 'Is good,' she announced, taking up a spoon and offering Alexandra a taste. 'Is favourite of Senhor O'Rourke.'

Alexandra swallowed the spoonful unwillingly, not wishing to offend her. It burned her throat like fire, it was so spicy, but it wasn't unpalatable, and she managed to make some complimentary comment which delighted Consuelo. However, she did manage to convey that she was not hungry enough to eat anything so filling, and Consuelo eventually agreed to make her an omelette. While the housekeeper was beating the eggs, Alexandra perched on a high stool nearby and said:

'Have you always worked for Senhor O'Rourke, Consuelo?'

The housekeeper shrugged. 'Since he come here, *senhorita*, yes. But when the *senhor's* father use the house, I work for him also.'

'Oh, yes.' Alexandra remembered what Clare had said about Declan's father.

'Senhor Declan's father—he build this house, *senhorita*.'
'Yes. Yes, I know.'

Consuelo turned to frown at her. 'Senhora Forman tell you?'

Alexandra's face gave her away. 'I—I think so.'

'Huh!' Consuelo turned back to the eggs, grumbling to herself. 'That woman—she is not welcome in my house!'

Alexandra closed her lips tightly. She would not ask why. But she didn't have to. Consuelo took her silence for acquiescence.

'She is always here,' she went on impatiently, 'making herself at home, behaving as if this were her house!'

Alexandra bit her lip. 'I—I expect she finds her own home rather different,' she ventured.

'Perhaps, perhaps!' Consuelo gestured angrily. 'But she chose to come out here—running after Senhor Declan! A married woman! And herself the wife of the priest!'

Alexandra didn't know what to say. Consuelo's words had shocked her, she couldn't deny that, and yet they were only what she had half expected to hear. Almost without volition she was involved in this discussion, and her whole system curled with distaste.

'I—I'm sure it's nothing like that——' she began, but Consuelo shook her head.

'You do not understand, *senhorita*. Senhor Declan knew Senhora Forman in São Paulo. Before she was—Senhora Forman.'

Alexandra drew an unsteady breath. 'It's—really nothing to do with me, Consuelo,' she murmured.

Consuelo sniffed. 'You think it is right?'

'I didn't say that.' Alexandra sought for words. 'I only meant—perhaps you're imagining——'

'Consuelo does not imagine this.' She tipped oil into a frying pan and waited for it to smoke. 'But you are right. I should not gossip. Senhor Declan, would be most angry. He does not—how you say it?—he does not care what people think.'

Alexandra sighed, wishing she could change the subject. 'Er—tell me—tell me about yourself, Consuelo. Are you married? Do you have any family?'

Consuelo was silent for so long that Alexandra thought she was not going to answer her, but at last she said: '*Nao, senhorita.* I did not marry. I was—how you say?—nurse to Senhor Declan?'

'Nurse?' Alexandra frowned. 'He was ill?'

Consuelo shook her head vigorously. '*Nao, nao!*' She gestured. 'To the little boy he was.'

'Oh—nursemaid.'

'*Sim*, nursemaid,' Consuelo nodded agreeably. 'I live in São Paulo, too. But when Senhor Declan is coming here—I come, too.'

'I see.' Watching Consuelo pour the beaten eggs into the pan Alexandra wondered how she was going to manage to eat anything after what Consuelo had told her about Clare Forman. But she forced these thoughts away and returned to her theme: 'You didn't—mind the isolation?'

'*Nao, senhorita.* I have plenty to do. I care for the house, I make the meals, I look after Senhor Declan. Sometimes I do sewing, and sometimes I go with him to the village to help the little ones. Is a good life.'

'Yes.' Alexandra digested this. 'And—and have you been here long?'

Consuelo considered this, watching the eggs in the pan. 'Maybe three—four years. I do not remember exactly, *senhorita*. Senhor Declan, he work for time in hospital in São Paulo, you understand? Then he say he is coming here.' She gave a faint, reminiscent smile. 'His father, he was *so* angry! And his mother . . .' She sighed. 'She was sad. She love her son so much. She not want him to go so far away.'

'He—he's an only child, then?'

Consuelo looked up and actually chuckled. 'Ay, ay, *nao, senhorita.* The *senhor*, he has six sisters!'

'Six?' Alexandra stared at her. 'Good lord!'

Consuelo looked back at the pan. 'Is good, *senhorita*. Children bring much happiness. Is sad all girls, *sim*, but is the will of God!'

Alexandra gave a helpless shrug of her shoulders. 'I have no brothers or sisters.'

'I know.' Consuelo looked sympathetic. 'But perhaps one day, hmm?'

Alexandra's brows drew together. 'I hardly think that's likely, Consuelo. My mother is dead.'

'*Sim, senhorita,* I know. Your father, he stay with us for time when not on—how you say—expedition?'

'I see,' Alexandra nodded.

'But he may marry again,' went on Consuelo cheerfully. 'Is good to have wife and children.'

'I don't think my father would do that,' replied Alexandra, somewhat stiffly, but as she said the words she couldn't help but wonder how true they were. How could she be sure what her father would or would not do? She hardly knew him, she realised with a start. For years he had been someone she had seen at holiday times, and apart from those times she didn't know how he conducted his life. He was still quite a young man, in his forties, she supposed. It wasn't beyond the realms of possibility that he might marry again, and yet the idea had never occurred to her until now ...

Consuelo served the omelette with a crisp salad, offered fruit as a dessert, and made coffee. Alexandra seated herself beside the fire in the living room and ate from a tray on her knees. The light meal was delicious and she managed to eat sufficient to waylay any comments Consuelo might have made. Afterwards, she lingered over her coffee, trying to absorb the contents of a book on butterflies, but when nine-thirty came and went and there was still no sign of Declan she decided to go to bed.

She bade Consuelo goodnight and went to her room where her lamp had been lit in her absence. Then she sat for a while on the edge of her bed wondering why it was that anything concerning Declan O'Rourke should have become so important to her.

She slept much better that night. She didn't bother with a nightgown, and the cool cotton sheets were much less cumbersome. Such dreams as she had did not disturb her, and she awakened next morning feeling infinitely more refreshed. When she did open her eyes, however, she had the distinct impression that someone, or something, had awakened her, and memories of the tarantula were strong in her mind as she struggled uneasily into a sitting position, holding the sheets very firmly beneath her chin.

But there was no apparent sign of any unwelcome visitor and she was about to slide her legs out of bed when her door was opened a few inches and Declan put his head round.

Horrified, she slid down the bed again, and his expression mocked her as he said: 'I did knock, but you didn't answer.'

So that was what had woken her, she thought with relief. 'I—I was asleep,' she murmured awkwardly. 'What do you want?'

He came fully into the room. 'I came to examine your bite,' he remarked, standing before her, hands on his hips, lean and handsome in navy cotton pants and a collarless cotton sweat shirt.

'Well, you can't do it now.' Alexandra was panic-stricken. It was one thing to accept that he was a doctor, and quite another to have him examine her without any warning.

His expression hardened. 'Why not? I thought we'd got over all that.'

'We have—at least—oh, *please*!'

She rolled over, burying her hot face in the pillow, and he seemed to repent. 'Okay,' he said dryly. 'I also came to ask whether you considered yourself sufficiently recovered from your first trip to attempt another venture into the jungle.'

'W—what?' She rolled over again slowly.

'I'm going to visit a village about five miles away. I thought you might like to come.'

Alexandra wriggled up on to her pillows. 'In—in the station wagon?'

He shook his head. 'I'm afraid not. No roads.'

'Not—walking?'

'No, not that either. Do you ride?'

'Well, I have,' she conceded slowly. 'But I'm not very good at it.' She couldn't tell him that she was afraid of horses!

However, Declan didn't seem to find her answer in any way reluctant. 'That's all right, then,' he said. 'Do you want to come?'

Alexandra hesitated. The prospect of spending a whole day in his company was tempting, although she had the feeling that she would have more sense if she stayed away from him.

'I—is Mrs. Forman coming, too?'

His eyes darkened. 'Do you want me to do something violent, like ripping that sheet off you?' he demanded. 'Because that's what you're asking for!'

Alexandra moved her shoulders apologetically. 'I—would like to come, but——'

'But what?'

'You won't—expect too much of me, will you?'

He half turned away, supporting himself against the door. 'I could ask the same of you, couldn't I?' he commented dryly. 'Oh, get dressed and get something to eat. I have to collect my equipment.'

'All right.' Alexandra half propped herself up on her elbows. 'Declan——'

'Yes.' He was impatient to be gone now.

'Have you had—any further news about my father?'

He paused in the doorway and looked at her. 'No, not yet. I may have, later today. One of my men is flying the jet up from Bogota.' He shrugged expressively. 'I'll let you know.'

Alexandra couldn't hide her indignation. 'You mean I could have flown to Bogota when this man did?'

He looked bored. 'Don't let's start that again.'

'I know, but——'

'Get dressed,' he advised irritably, and closed the door behind him.

This morning there was nothing more terrifying in the bathroom than a bright-eyed lizard that slithered away at her approach. The lizards didn't scare her. They always seemed quite friendly little creatures, and she watched it as she sluiced her face and cleaned her teeth. It was still early, she realised, as she dressed in jeans and a blue denim shirt. Not yet eight o'clock. But she had gone to bed early the night before and she didn't feel at all sleepy now.

Consuelo had left some warm rolls, a dish of conserve, and a jug of coffee on the dining table. Alexandra helped herself, enjoying the scents from the garden—the perfume of the flowers, the spicy fragrance of herbs, and the rough earthy smell of damp soil. She felt rather excited at the prospect of leaving the confines of the house again, and she refused to consider the disasters that might lie ahead of her.

Declan reappeared as she was finishing her second cup of coffee. 'Are you ready?' he asked, surveying her with cool appraisal.

Alexandra wiped her mouth on a napkin. 'Yes. Do I need a coat?'

'I should take a jacket for later,' he agreed, nodding.

'Consuelo will provide you with a gaucho hat.'

'A gaucho hat?'

'That's right. It helps keep your head cool.' He looked down at her sandal-shod feet. 'And boots, needless to say.'

The stables were at the back of the house. The dogs were housed here too and Alexandra looked about her with interest. The wooden fence surrounded the property, but behind the house the undergrowth had been cleared and tall grasses moved in the breeze that blew down from the mountains above them. There were four horses in the stables, sturdy, strong-limbed animals with broad feet to find a secure footing on the mountainous slopes. An Indian boy had charge of the animals, and Declan explained that he and his brothers from a nearby village exercised them regularly.

Alexandra's horse was a chestnut mare, small and amiable, unmoved by the excitability of the wolfhounds. Alexandra managed to hide the panic that stiffened her when it came and nuzzled her shoulder. If she wasn't afraid of the dogs, why should this placid animal disturb her?

'I don't think you'll have any trouble with Rosina,' remarked Declan, waiting for her to mount before swinging himself up on to the back of a broad black stallion. 'She's a gentle creature. My sisters have ridden her without any trouble, and one of them is about your age.'

Alexandra looked at him out of the corners of her eyes, and then, with a convulsive swallow, she put her foot in the stirrup and swung herself into the mare's saddle. Rosina moved a little protestingly but then was still, and quivering, Alexandra said: 'I—I'm ready.'

Declan's dark brows had drawn closer together, but he said nothing, merely mounted his own animal and asked the stable boy to restrain the dogs and open the gate in the fence. They emerged on to the mountainside, just above the house, where stubbly trees strove to survive, and the rushing waters of the ravine were that much louder.

For a moment Alexandra forgot her fears in the pure delight of the view that now confronted her. The sparse undergrowth fell away to the rim of the chasm, sun-shadowed, the rocks all shades from pale green, and blue, to deepest purple. Beyond the ravine the forest rose up again towards the cloudless sky, the sun a metallic blur as it crept towards its zenith.

Declan allowed her a moment to just sit and absorb, and then he turned his horse and began to move away. Rosina followed him, and Alexandra tightened the knot of her broad-brimmed hat with one hand and held tightly to the reins with the other. She was sweating already, but it was more from fear than anything else. She hoped the placid Rosina could not sense the puny cowardice of the girl on her back.

They were following a path which seemed to be leading down towards the brink of the ravine, and Alexandra's throat felt dry. Even the most undemanding of steeds required some sort of control and she knew that if Rosina panicked so would she.

Declan half turned in his saddle at that moment, looking back at her, one leg draped around his pommel to make the action more comfortable. 'Are you all right?' he enquired, and she nodded urgently, not wanting him to notice how pale she must be looking.

He shrugged and turned round again, calling: 'Don't worry. We're not taking the track down the ravine—not today anyway. We follow this path down for a short way, and then it takes us up and over that bluff—can you see?'

He pointed ahead, and Alexandra nodded. But then realising he could not see her gesture of acquiescence, she managed to call: 'Yes, I can see.'

Casting another strange glance back at her, Declan adjusted his posture as the black began the steep descent to where the path forked. Following him, Alexandra was amazed that the horses did not slip or slide on the rocky surface, but obviously they were used to going this way and needed little encouragement. Alexandra closed her eyes. The sight of the ravine on her left and the possibilities imaginable if Rosina should miss her footing did not bear thinking about.

'What the hell are you doing?'

Declan's harsh voice broke into her silent prayers, and she opened her eyes to find that he had stopped at the fork and was looking back at her angrily.

'I—I was nervous—of the ravine,' she stammered.

'Haven't you the sense to know that on paths like these a rider needs to keep all his wits about him? What if Rosina lost her footing?'

Alexandra tensed. 'What if she did? What could I do about it?'

'Well, if you don't know then you shouldn't be on a bloody horse!' he swore angrily.

'Perhaps I shouldn't at that!' she retorted.

Declan's face darkened. 'I'll take you back——'

'No!' Alexandra was contrite. 'No—please!' In spite of her fears she wanted to go on. 'I'm sorry, I was—stupid. I won't do it again.'

'Won't you?' Declan glared at her. 'How can I believe you?'

Alexandra hunched her shoulders frustratedly. 'What do you want me to say and I'll say it!' she exclaimed, and was chilled by the sudden cold anger in his eyes. All at once she remembered what Clare Forman had said about a certain ruthlessness he possessed. Looking at him now she could believe it.

He made no answer but swung his horse up the track that led over the bluff, leaving her to follow him or go back alone. The black moved swiftly up the slope and Alexandra was forced, much against her better judgement, to spur

Rosina on to keep up with him.

But beyond the bluff, the panorama made her draw swiftly on the reins, bringing the mare to an abrupt halt. Miles and miles of undulating country was spread out before her, miles of forests and rocky scrubland, ragged hills and mountainous peaks. Here and there the sun glinted on stretches of water, lakes caught in the folds of the landscape like jewels in green velvet. Overhead, wheeling and gliding, swept a group of falcons whose habitat this high valley must be.

Declan looked back and saw the enchanted expression on her face and as though relenting his earlier anger, he rode back to her. 'Well?' he challenged. 'Was it worth the effort?'

Alexandra moved her shoulders helplessly. 'I never dreamed—we seemed so remote!'

'Make no mistake,' remarked Declan dryly, 'we are! Don't let the beauty of the valley blind you to that fact. There is no civilisation here as you know it. But the soil is good, and the crops grow. These people are lucky.'

'People?' Alexandra was confused. 'But where are the people?'

'You'll see them.' Declan pointed ahead. 'The trees hide the villages very successfully. But they're there. These people used to live much deeper into the jungle, nearer the river, but gradually they've made their way up here. They're a mixture of Indians and *caboclos*, half Christian, half pagan.'

'*Caboclos?* What are they?'

'Half Indian, half Portuguese,' replied Declan laconically. 'Like my father!'

If he had intended to shock her, she refused to be shocked. All the same, some three-quarters of an hour later, when they descended between trees to a village which lay on the banks of a narrow stream, she couldn't help but

101

contrast his sophistication with the primitiveness of this settlement.

She was hot now, very hot. The sun was almost completely overhead, and her clothes were clinging to her. Their journey had taken them along a narrow ridge, exposed to the heat of the sun, and only now as they plunged among trees did she appreciate why the Indians built their homes in the shade.

Declan was welcomed enthusiastically. Children ran to grasp his bridle, chattering excitedly until they saw Alexandra and then they fell back to hide shyly behind their mothers. Alexandra herself was relieved to see that the men were decently covered, and as she was gradually growing used to seeing the women she could at least control the colour that was apt to flood her cheeks.

Declan stopped beside an elderly man, probably the headman of the village, Alexandra decided, and dismounted. They greeted one another warmly, shaking hands, and then Declan indicated that Alexandra should dismount also. Their arrival had aroused a certain amount of curiosity and Alexandra was aware that she was the focal point.

She climbed down rather awkwardly, afraid that Rosina might shy unexpectedly and overbalance her. But she accomplished the feat without incident and was startled when Declan grasped her wrist in a firm hold and drew her forward.

'This is Tempest's daughter,' he said to the old man, speaking English very slowly. 'You remember Tempest?'

The old man nodded, his eyes on the girl. He was a terrifying figure to someone as unused to these people as Alexandra, and she had to force herself not to flinch when he reached out a horny hand and touched the softness of her hair.

'Tempest's daughter,' he said, in guttural tones. 'I remember.'

102

He was very thin. The skin clung to his rib-cage, and his limbs were skeletal. But it was his face which horrified her most. A hideous mask of tattooing covered his cheekbones, and his nostrils were elongated as if they had been torn by some animal. She realised now why Declan was keeping his hold on her wrist. Without his silent insistence she might easily have drawn back.

Declan looked at her. 'Rubez,' he said, by way of an introduction. 'Once chief of the Ayala tribe.'

Alexandra bit her lip. Was she expected to say something? 'How—how do you do?' she managed unevenly. 'You—you know my father?'

The old man smiled, at least she assumed the grotesque twisting of his lips was a smile. He nodded again. 'Tempest,' he said. 'The medicine man.'

'Medicine man?' Alexandra looked blankly at Declan.

His eyes adjured her not to argue. 'That's right,' he said. 'The medicine man.'

The introductions were over and Rubez summoned the women. A group of three approached shyly, and he directed that Alexandra should go with them. Alexandra cast a protesting look in Declan's direction, but he made no move to help her, his expression vaguely impatient. She realised that this was expected of her and yet she still felt resentful. He must know that she was on edge and nervous and yet he offered no assistance. Instead, he walked away with the elderly tribesman towards a hut set apart from the others.

The women took charge of Alexandra. Giggling and chattering together, they coaxed her with them to a larger hut, a sort of communal living room, she guessed. There were hammocks slung in rows along the walls and domestic animals wandered in and out at will. The women indicated that Alexandra should sit down on the rush mats on the floor and presently an enormous iron cooking pot was produced containing a stew very much like the one Consuelo had been preparing the night before. She was passed an earthenware bowl and some of the stew was ladled into it. Obviously she was expected to share their simple meal, and with some misgivings she raised the bowl to her lips.

Apart from the fact that it was very spicy, and burned her mouth, it was not at all bad, and she managed to smile and by means of gesticulation express her enjoyment. The women smiled in return, and moved closer, clearly fascinated by the long swathe of corn-coloured hair and her fair skin. Alexandra steeled herself not to feel alarm at the press of humanity that surrounded her, but the heat of their bodies was almost overwhelming in the confinement of the hut.

She was on the point of scrambling to her feet and making an ungainly exit when Declan and the chief reappeared in the open doorway. She was desperately glad to see them, and her relief must have shown in her face. The women noticed and nodded and pointed at Declan, almost as though they imagined there to be something between them. And when Alexandra saw the wry twist to Declan's mouth she guessed she wasn't far wrong.

But at least she was allowed to stand up, and she crossed the room to his side on rather unsteady legs. She had the sense not to say how relieved she was to see him, and he said something to the women which obviously delighted them.

It was wonderful to emerge into the sunlight again, although the heat made Alexandra feel weak. Declan was bidding their host goodbye, and wiping the sweat from her forehead she slid her hat back on to her head. Her shirt was clinging to her and she pulled the material away from her skin, conscious of the way the cloth outlined her rounded breasts. The horses were brought for them and Declan put the pack containing his medical equipment in his saddle-bag. Alexandra mounted the mare almost eagerly, unutterably relieved to be on their way again.

They rode south out of the village, the opposite way from when they came in. She hoped that didn't mean they would be returning this way later in the day. They followed a track beside the stream where flowers grew in clusters, pink and lilac and palest blue, the lazy droning of the insects hanging heavily in the languid air.

'Where are we going?' she ventured at last when the village had dropped far behind. 'It's so hot!'

Declan glanced back at her. 'Would you like to rest for a while?'

'Could we?'

'You were supposed to have rested in the village.'

'What? I was scrutinised like an insect under a microscope!'

He raised dark eyebrows. 'Only by the women,' he conceded.

'Only!'

'You'd have liked it less if Rubez had offered you to his tribesmen.'

Alexandra was silent for a while. 'Was that likely?' she asked at last, in a small voice.

Declan half smiled. 'No. No, it was not. However, it is customary for an Indian to offer his wife to a passing traveller.'

Alexandra gasped, 'You mean—you—you——'

Declan's expression hardened. 'No, I do not mean that at all. My God, what a sordid little mind you've got!'

Alexandra coloured hotly. 'I only meant——'

'I know what you meant!'

Declan swung round and ignored her protests. He spurred the black into a canter and she was soon left far behind. Sweat was pouring out of her as she dug her heels into Rosina's sides in an effort to speed the mare up, but Rosina seemed unwilling to hurry. Behind her dark glasses, Alexandra's eyes felt hot and gritty, and a dull ache was beginning near her temples.

Then, without warning, a snake uncurled from behind a rock in front of them, darting across their path with a curious chattering sound. Alexandra was petrified. She guessed it was a rattlesnake and its bite was deadly to both horse and man. Rosina realised it too, and with a startled whinny, she reared on her hind legs, almost unseating her rider. But Alexandra clung on desperately, a scream escaping from her lips as the snake coiled ready to spring.

Rosina was out of control now. She sensed Alexandra's panic and that added to her own was enough to send her wild with frenzy. She turned and ploughed across the stream, stumbling on the stones, soaking Alexandra in the process. Not that she cared. She was too busy hanging on for dear life. She thought she could hear Declan shouting her name, but she couldn't be sure, and besides, beyond the stream there were rocky outcrops with only goat paths to follow, and Rosina was thundering towards them, apparently uncaring of her own limitations.

CHAPTER SEVEN

FORTUNATELY perhaps for Alexandra, she was thrown before Rosina reached the rocks, and she fell heavily on to the scrubby turf, winded but not unconscious. She lay there for several minutes with her eyes closed, scarcely able to believe that her headlong flight was over, and then blinked in surprise when Declan came galloping up to her and leapt from his horse beside her. He dropped down on to his knees, supporting her head with his arm, and asked huskily: 'Dear heaven, are you all right?'

Alexandra swallowed with difficulty, deeply disturbed by the concern in his blue eyes. 'Y-yes,' she stammered, 'I'm fine.' She raised a hand to shade her eyes. Her glasses must have been lost in the fall. 'It was the rattlesnake. Rosina . . .'

'Rosina will be okay. I'll go after her in a few minutes. She panicked. I saw it all.' Declan's voice roughened. 'Are you sure you're not hurt, Alexandra?'

Alexandra tried to struggle into a sitting position, but her head was throbbing quite badly now and she winced.

'What is it?' he demanded, his intent eyes raking her slender form. 'You are hurt!'

'No.' She managed to sit up without his support. She rubbed the back of her hand across her forehead, hiding an awful sense of emotionalism. 'I—I've got a headache, that's all.'

Declan sat back on his heels, surveying her silently for a minute, and then he got to his feet. He went to his horse

107

and took a bottle of tablets out of the saddlebag.

'Here,' he said, holding out two. 'Can you take them without water, or would you like a drink?'

'A drink?' Alexandra licked her lips. 'Do you have something?'

'Only beer, I'm afraid. Will that do?'

She nodded eagerly. 'Oh, yes. I'm—parched.'

The warm beer had never tasted so good and while she drank Declan whistled back the frightened mare. She came slowly, encouraged by the sound of his voice, and Declan fastened her reins to those of the black. Then he collected Alexandra's thrown hat and glasses, grimacing when he found the lenses smashed.

'I think we'll rest for a while before going on,' he said, coming back to her. 'But not here. It's shadier on the other side of the stream.'

Alexandra shuddered. 'The rattlesnake——'

'——will be long gone. Besides, I'm not suggesting we stay near the rocks. A few yards further on there's a small pool. It will be cooler there.' He stood looking down at her. 'Can you mount the mare or would you rather walk?'

Alexandra sighed, looking warily at Rosina. 'I think I'd rather walk.'

'Okay.' Declan gathered the black's reins. 'You're sure you can make it?'

'Oh, of course.' Alexandra refused to let him see how shaken she was. She got to her feet, brushing herself down, and as she did so she felt a sharp pain in her shoulder. She caught her breath, turning away so that he should not notice, and Declan nodded towards the stream.

'Come on. It's shallow enough, fortunately. We can cross just over here. Your legs are pretty wet already.'

Alexandra couldn't prevent a shudder as they climbed the bank on the other side of the stream, but there was no sign now of the rattler. The sun was beating down unmercifully as they delved deeper into the trees and finally came upon the pool Declan had mentioned. Fern-fringed and placid, it looked very inviting, huge lotus lilies floating on its surface.

Declan dragged the roll from the back of his saddle and spread it out in the shade. It was a quilted sleeping bag and made a comfortable covering for them to sit on. Alexandra dropped down on to it gladly, relieved to be off legs which had grown steadily more uncertain.

Declan did not immediately sit down but wandered to the water's edge, looking down into the depths. His back was turned and Alexandra gingerly slid her fingers inside the collar of her shirt and felt tentatively over her shoulder. She winced as she touched the abrasion which was causing her such pain each time the material of her shirt rubbed against it and saw to her dismay that there was blood on her fingers when she drew them away.

Declan was coming back and she rubbed her hands quickly against the turf, erasing the traces of blood. Her face was averted and she hoped he would not notice her confusion. But the last thing she could cope with right now was for him to touch her. She didn't quite know why she felt so strongly about it, but she knew that the shock of seeing the rattlesnake combined with that jarring fall from her horse had left her feeling hopelessly vulnerable. She didn't want his kindness, his *sympathy*! The trouble was, she didn't know what she did want.

Declan lowered his weight beside her, looking at her out of the corners of his eyes. 'I suppose I should apologise,' he said quietly.

Alexandra's head jerked up. 'Why?'

'Well, if I hadn't ridden off like that, the whole incident might never have happened.'

She shook her head, looking away from him. 'Accidents happen. They're nobody's fault. If—if I'd been able to control Rosina . . .'

'No one can control a horse maddened by fear. It was best to let her have her head. A more experienced rider might have avoided being thrown, that's all.'

Alexandra bent her head. 'And I'm not very experienced.'

'I had gathered that.' Declan frowned. 'In fact, I'd say you were not experienced at all.'

Alexandra shrugged, and then wished she hadn't as her shoulder protested painfully. 'I—I—horses used to frighten me.'

Declan's mouth turned down at the corners. 'Used to?' he chided. 'I think they still do.' He shook his head. 'Why didn't you tell me you were nervous?'

Alexandra flicked a blade of grass from the leg of her jeans. 'I manage,' she replied defensively.

'Umm.' Declan stretched his length lazily, shading his eyes with his arm. 'Well, perhaps this little incident has taught you that in circumstances like these, one needs to be able to do a little more than just manage!'

Alexandra moved so that he should not see the blood which she was sure must have stained the shoulder of her shirt. She stared broodingly towards the pool. The prospect of the journey home appalled her, and she wondered with a sense of dread whether he had any other calls to make.

Declan had closed his eyes, but now they opened to regard her impatiently. 'Why are you looking so worried?' he exclaimed. 'I promise, I won't ride off and leave you again —no matter what comments you make!'

Alexandra held up her head. 'I—I wasn't thinking about that.'

'Then what were you thinking?'

She hesitated. 'Thoughts.'

He sighed. 'What thoughts?'

Alexandra bit her lip. 'Oh, well, if you must know, I was

110

wondering—I was wondering——' She sought about desperately for something to say. '—I wondered where the Indians—buried their dead.'

'Oh, really?' Declan sounded sceptical. He sat up, drawing up one knee to rest his arm upon it. 'Well, they don't.'

Alexandra stared at him in surprise. 'What do you mean?'

'Just what I say. They don't bury their dead.'

Alexandra, to whom this had been just a flash of inspiration, was now totally involved. 'What do they do, then?'

Declan shrugged. 'There are various rituals, but being buried is, to an Indian, a barbarous act. Dead bodies are usually exposed in trees until the bones are picked clean, or burned. The dry bones are crushed afterwards to powder and mixed with something like mashed banana and eaten.'

Alexandra felt sick. 'Eaten?'

'Yes, eaten. To an Indian the threat of his bones not being consumed condemns him to an afterlife of restless wandering. A sort of unclean spirit, we might say.'

'But—but that's cannibalism!' Alexandra made an impotent gesture. 'How can they?'

Declan unfastened the buttons of his shirt and rubbed the rough hair on his chest. 'I guess they'd find some of the things we do pretty peculiar.'

Alexandra dragged her eyes away from him. His skin was brown and smooth, slightly moist now from the heat of his body. The hair on the back of his neck was damp, too, and clung to his scalp, thick and straight. He made her wholly aware of herself, of her body and its awakening needs, a thing no one else had ever done. It was a new and disturbing experience.

'Aren't you going to rest?' he asked, and she was forced to look round at him.

'Oh, I—I am resting,' she stammered.

His eyes darkened suddenly, and his jaw was taut. 'Stop it, Alexandra,' he ground out harshly.

111

'Stop what? I don't know what you mean.'

'Yes, you do.' His eyes dropped meaningfully to the opened vee of her shirt. 'I don't think your father would approve.'

'You're imagining things!' Alexandra's cheeks burned. 'Can't I even look at you?'

Declan sighed. 'Not like that. No.'

Alexandra hunched her shoulders. 'I'm sorry.'

Declan uttered a harsh imprecation. 'What is it you want, Alexandra? Experimentation—or experience?'

She looked down at her knees. 'I've had experiences with men!' she declared defensively.

'Have you? Like you've had experience with horses, I suppose.'

'That's not fair!' Her eyes were stormy. 'I'm not a child, you know.'

'Aren't you? And do you want me to prove that?'

She trembled. 'How?'

His mouth twisted. 'It seems to me that there is only one way.' His hand curved over the nape of her neck under her hair. 'Come here.'

Alexandra's throat felt choked. The feel of his fingers against her neck was a tantalising pleasure, and she moved her shoulders to increase the awareness, not really feeling the pain at that moment. He moved closer to her, and she felt the warmth of his breath against her ear as his other hand cupped her throat and slid down over the shirt, his knuckles lingering against her breasts so that she had the irresistible urge to press herself against him. His hands gripped her waist, turning her towards him, and her eyes flickered upward to his, her lips parting invitingly.

'God, *no*!'

His abrupt rejection of her was absolute. He sprang to his feet, pushing her away from him so roughly that she fell back against the sleeping bag. Her groan of agony was unmistakable, arresting his attention when he was about to stride away from her. His eyes narrowed, and he turned uncomprehendingly, thrusting his hands into his trousers pockets.

'Did I hurt you?' he demanded in harsh disbelief.

Alexandra couldn't answer him. The stinging pain in her shoulder was causing the tears to well up in her eyes, rolling unheeded down her pale cheeks. She lay there mutely, moving her head slowly from side to side, but he did not believe her. He came down beside her, his eyes dark with anger.

'What in hell is the matter?' he swore. 'What did I do?' He caught her by the shoulders, enraged enough to shake the truth out of her, and she whimpered in anguish.

A dawning understanding drew his dark brows together. He could feel the sticky dampness beneath his fingers. With his teeth clamped fiercely together he gently rolled her over and saw the darkening stain just above her left shoulder-blade.

'Why didn't you tell me?' he exhorted savagely. 'My God, haven't I asked you to tell me if you so much as scratch yourself, and you were going to hide *this*!'

'I—I wasn't. I'd have told you——'

He turned her on to her side. 'When?' He began unbuttoning her shirt, pushing aside her protesting fingers.

'When—when we got back.'

He drew her shirt off her shoulder, taking care not to pull the torn skin more than was necessary. 'Why not now?'

Alexandra made a helpless movement of her hand, overwhelmingly conscious of his nearness. 'I—I didn't want you to touch me,' she admitted, too disturbed to dissemble.

He tipped his head to look at her. 'Why not?'

'Don't you know that, too?' she asked bitterly.

His eyes darkened and without another word he got to his feet and walked across to where his horse was standing beneath the trees. He took his pack from the saddlebag and brought it back to where she was lying, opening it and taking out some salve and a pad of lint. Then he knelt beside her again, cleaning the scrape with spirit before applying the salve. Alexandra flinched only once, when the spirit stung her flesh, but then lay obediently while he applied the salve and fastened the pad of lint in position with strips of plaster. Then he drew her shirt back into position and fastened the buttons.

Alexandra let him do as he willed. She felt totally incapable of any sensible speech, and there was an awful sense of inadequacy sinking her stomach. What must he be thinking of her? she thought dispiritedly. And what of this would he tell her father when Professor Tempest and his assistant returned to Paradiablo? Declan sat on the sleeping bag beside her, putting the tube of salve, the spirit and the roll of plaster back into his pack. Then he tossed the leather satchel aside and looked down at her.

'Does that feel better?' he asked.

Alexandra nodded, pushing herself up. 'Yes, thank you.' She pressed her lips together for a moment. 'I—I suppose I ought to apologise now.'

His mouth twisted. 'That's not necessary.'

'Isn't it?' She looked sideways at him. 'Will you tell my father?'

He sighed, running a hand over the hair at the back of his neck. 'No.'

She couldn't leave it. 'I thought you would.'

'Why?' He sounded as though she was beginning to annoy him again.

'I—I just thought—as you find me so—so infuriating . . .'

'Did I say that?'

'You didn't have to say anything.' She looked down at her hands. 'You can even—you can even take—take my clothes off without it meaning anything to you!'

'Stop talking such bloody drivel!' he snapped angrily. 'What would you have had me do? You'd have been scared out of your wits if I'd so much as touched you!'

'I wouldn't!' She was indignant.

'Look, Alexandra, I don't know if this is some sort of game you play at that school of yours, but I'm warning you I'm no schoolboy, and much more of this and you'll land yourself in deep trouble.' He was glaring furiously at her as he spoke but something in her expression tempered his anger. 'Oh, Alexandra, you're a beautiful girl. Okay, I know it. In a couple of years your father will have every male in the district beating a path to your door to contend with, but right now——'

'Right now?'

He stared into her eyes. 'Right now—right now——' He gave a grimace of self-disgust. 'Oh, God, Alexandra, I'm only human!'

He captured one of her hands and raised it to his mouth, pressing his lips to the palm with urgent insistence. She allowed her fingers to move against his cheek, and he drew them down on to his chest. His hand cupped her throat, his thumb tipping back her head. He lowered his mouth to her cheek and she felt a ripple of anticipation slide up her spine. Then his mouth moved across her soft skin until it covered hers, and all previous sexual encounters were as nothing compared to the tumult he aroused in her. His mouth hardened as he felt her response, his lips forcing hers apart as he bore her back against the sleeping bag, the weight of his body both a pleasure and a pain.

He kissed her many times, long, urgent kisses that weakened her resistance, destroyed any defence she might try to raise against him. Declan was no inexperienced teenager, he was a man, a man moreover committed to showing her exactly how dangerous loveplay could be. His mouth was hard and passionate, his caresses sent her senses spinning, and the evidence of his desire in the hard strength of his thighs was a potent stimulant.

Lethargy was creeping over her. They were so beautifully isolated here, they might have been in a world of their own. The only sounds were those of the birds and the insects, and occasionally the distant grunt of a forest animal. These forests had been here for a hundred million years, unmarked by the glaciers which had destroyed the northern hemisphere, and no doubt they would be here long after the world as she knew it had passed away. It was like a time out of mind, without past or future ...

Her body yielded beneath his, inviting his possession, but when his fingers touched the button at the waistband of her trousers she couldn't go through with it. With a little cry, she pushed his hand away, and he rolled on to his back to cover his forehead with his arms.

His eyes were closed and Alexandra clenched her fists impotently. It was no good. He was right, she was inexperienced, and while some yearning part of her system longed for his possession, that foolish, childish inhibition thrust itself between them.

She wanted desperately to tell him how she felt, to explain that she was not the prude he must be thinking her, but when she put out a tentative hand and touched his firm midriff he jack-knifed into a sitting position, pushing her hand away. He hunched his shoulders, his legs drawn up, in a position of complete exhaustion. Then, after a minute, he straightened and said: 'Get up. We're leaving.'

Alexandra opened her mouth to speak and then closed it again. What was the use? But she had to try. 'I'm—I'm sorry,' she ventured.

He looked at her with cold mockery as he got to his feet. 'I'm not.'

She raised dull eyes to his. 'Why not?'

'I never intended to seduce you, little girl!' he retorted, and his smile was not pleasant. 'If I had, you wouldn't have been able to stop me!'

'But—but——' She scrambled to her feet. 'You—you were—well, you tried to——'

He turned away. 'I just wanted to see how far that veneer of experience would take you,' he replied scornfully.

'I—I see.' Alexandra felt totally humiliated. 'I—I think you're despicable!'

He gave her a resigned stare. 'Put on your hat and get on your horse, and next time you want to play games, find someone of your own weight!'

The journey back to Paradiablo was conducted almost completely in silence. Alexandra was too absorbed with her own thoughts to speak and Declan seemed wholly remote. They rode back through the shallower slopes of the valley, seldom leaving the shade of the trees until the sun began to slide down the sky. Then they mounted the track out of the valley, crossed the ridge and began the descent down to the ravine where the paths forked.

It was almost dark when they reached the house, circling it to reach the rear entrance. The dogs were barking excitedly, able to hear their approach long before anyone else, but the stableboy was there to open the gates.

Declan dismounted with lithe, easy grace, making a fuss of the dogs, his good humour apparently restored. Alexandra climbed down more slowly. The long day had taken its toll of her and she felt as though she ached in every bone. She thought longingly of a bath and bed in that order, and she was quite prepared to suffer Declan's sarcasm to achieve them. She walked ahead of him along the side of the house, unconsciously inhaling the fragrance of the night-blooming stocks, and came to an abrupt halt at the sight of Clare Forman lounging in a chair on the verandah. Oh, no, she thought wearily, not tonight!

But there was no mistaking the other girl's flaming hair, and conscious of Declan not far behind her, Alexandra went on with infinite reluctance. Then she saw that Clare was not alone. A thin, fair-haired man was sitting beside her, a pale-faced man with a gentle, almost ascetic manner. Alexandra did not have to be told that this was the Reverend David Forman.

Clare saw her first and a strange, questioning look crossed her face as her eyes took in Alexandra's somewhat dishevelled appearance, the tangled disorder of her hair.

'Well, well,' she remarked mockingly, 'you've had quite a day, haven't you?'

Hearing his wife's voice, David Forman got to his feet and came to the verandah rail. His smile was reassuringly warming. 'You must be Alexandra,' he said, holding out his hand to help her up the steps. 'I'm David Forman, Clare's husband.'

Alexandra allowed him to assist her and came up beside them as Declan appeared round the side of the house. He seemed not at all perturbed to find that he had two unexpected visitors, and it was Clare this time who got out of her seat to welcome him.

'We've invited ourselves for supper, darling,' she informed him, with unconcealed intimacy. 'I knew you wouldn't mind.'

'Really, Clare, that's not true.' Apparently David Forman was less willing to accept reluctant hospitality, but Declan shook his head amiably.

'That's all right, Dave, honestly,' he smiled, shaking the other man's hand. 'How are you? It must be over a week since I've seen you.'

David smiled in return. 'Oh, I'm fine, Declan. And you?' He glanced round at Alexandra. 'I've been introducing myself to your guest.'

Declan's eyes flickered over Alexandra enigmatically.

118

'Have you?' His eyes moved on to David. 'We've just spent the day in the Dariba valley.'

Clare pouted. 'But why didn't you tell me, Declan? I'd have loved to have joined you!'

Declan shrugged. 'Now, Clare, you're not that keen on visiting old Rubez' village. Besides, I thought you said you and Dave were going over to Maracuja.'

'We did,' put in David, offering Alexandra his chair which she politely refused. 'I'm afraid I've got some bad news for you from there.'

'Really, David, can't you wait until after we've eaten?' Clare exclaimed impatiently.

Declan ignored her. 'Go on,' he commanded quietly.

'Well——' David looked apologetically towards Alexandra. 'It's yellow fever, Declan. I don't know how badly the village is infected, but . . .' he shrugged, 'it's there.'

Declan threw down his pack of equipment and felt around in his pockets for his cheroots. Putting one between his teeth, he said: 'You're sure?'

David sighed. 'It was old Juan Meres, Declan. He must be all of sixty years old. The family were quite prepared for him to die.' He shook his head. 'He'd been ill, you see. The usual aches and pains. Nothing to indicate . . .' He hunched his shoulders and pushed his hands into the pockets of his khaki shorts. 'I was talking with him. He had a fever, but he was quite lucid. Then he vomited.' He lifted his shoulders expressively. 'There was blood——'

'Oh, honestly, David!' Clare's expression mirrored her disgust. 'Must you go into all the gory details? Declan knows the symptoms better than you do!'

Alexandra stood listening in silence. Her own feelings were disturbingly upsetting. The description David had given had not disgusted her, but the thought of Declan going to the village, of putting himself within reach of the deadly virus, did not bear thinking about.

119

She ran a trembling hand round the back of her neck, under the weight of her hair. If only she knew more about the disease. All she really knew was that Bob Haze had insisted on her being vaccinated against it before leaving England.

Declan had lit his cheroot and was staring thoughtfully down at the floor at his feet. Darkness was enveloping them like a cloak and Alexandra shivered. Suddenly the jungle was a dark and menacing place.

Declan looked up. 'I'll have to go,' he said with decision. 'How is Juan?'

David shook his head, and Declan nodded. 'I see.' He glanced round at all of them, his eyes flickering over Alexandra without emotion. 'I'm afraid you'll have to have that supper party without me. But I'm sure Consuelo ...'

'I'll come with you, Declan,' offered David, stepping forward, but Declan shook his head.

'I think not, Dave. Thanks anyway. I'll call at the mission at Vareja. The sisters have all been vaccinated, and as soon as they know ...' He sighed. 'Now, you'll excuse me, I'd like a shower and a change of clothes before leaving.'

Alexandra followed him into the living room, but he didn't stop to speak to her, and besides, Clare and David were close behind her.

'Well!' Clare was bitter. 'You really enjoyed that, didn't you, David?'

'Don't be silly, Clare.' David looked at Alexandra with appealing candour. 'I expect you'd like to bathe, too. Perhaps it would be better if Clare and I left——'

'No, please—stay!' Alexandra would never have believed that she would actually ask for Clare's company. 'I mean, I'm sure Declan would want you to.'

Clare's narrowed eyes registered Alexandra's use of Declan's given name. Her voice was mocking as she said: 'I'm sure he would.'

David was not at all devious. 'All right, thank you, Alexandra. I may call you that, may I not?'

'Of course.' Alexandra forced a smile. 'Now, if you'll excuse me for a few minutes, I'll go and—freshen up. Please, make yourselves comfortable. Have—have a drink.'

Leaving them to it, she went through the door into the dimly lit passage beyond. She hesitated outside Declan's door. She would have liked to have spoken to him before he left, to ask him to take care, to look after himself, but her fingers would not turn the handle.

She was still standing there when the door opened and Declan appeared, miraculously bathed and changed, his personal cleanliness a distinct contrast to hers. He paused in the doorway, looking down at her with narrowed eyes. 'Well?'

Alexandra linked and unlinked her fingers. 'I—I just wanted to say goodbye.'

'Goodbye.'

'Oh, Declan——' She bent her head. 'You—you will take care, won't you?'

'I'm a doctor, Alexandra. I always take care.' His voice was cool, impersonal.

She lifted her head. 'There—there's nothing I can do, is there? I mean—well, I have studied first aid——'

'No, thank you.'

'I'd like to help you, Declan.'

His mouth twisted. 'Would you? Then I suggest you have an early supper and go to bed. I shan't be back to-night.'

'You won't?' Her eyes were wide and questioning. 'When will you be back?'

'I hope, tomorrow. If not, have Consuelo dress your shoulder.'

'I can manage.' She was hurt by his indifference and unnecessarily abrupt.

121

'I said have Consuelo do it.' He caught her chin in one hand, and turned her face up to his. 'Stop feeling sorry for yourself. I don't want to hurt you, Alexandra, but if we go on like this, I will.'

She dragged herself away from him. 'I don't know what you mean.'

'Yes, you do.' He closed his door, and leaned back against it, his hand resting on the handle. 'All right, I found the conditions you were prepared to suffer in order to see your father unwillingly admirable. But since you came here, you've consistently tried my patience.'

'I think you like humiliating me,' she mumbled childishly.

'I don't. I'm trying to keep a balance between us. I realise it's difficult for you to adjust to the conditions, but I will not condone promiscuity!'

'You flatter yourself!'

'Do I? As I'm the only unattached male around, it's only natural that you should try your claws on me.'

Alexandra hunched her shoulders. 'And I suppose you're going to tell me that what happened this afternoon was all my fault!'

'Well, wasn't it?' He was ironic. 'Oh, I admit to having the usual quota of sexual urges, and I also admit that you aroused them, but——' he held her startled eyes with his: '—but they were never out of control. *Any* attractive female can do that to a man, or didn't you know?'

Alexandra turned away. 'I hate you, Declan O'Rourke!' she muttered.

'Good.' He straightened. 'Let's keep it that way, shall we?'

CHAPTER EIGHT

IT was almost a week before Alexandra saw Declan again.

Two days after his departure, he sent word that he was staying in Maracuja until he had discovered the extent of the epidemic, and that Alexandra should ask the Formans to come and stay with her at the house until he got back. An Indian boy brought the message, and when Alexandra showed it to Consuelo, she lost no time in voicing her disapproval.

'The *senhorita* is safe here with Consuelo,' she protested. 'What for you need the Formans?'

Alexandra forced a smile. The very last person she needed to see right now was Clare Forman. It was all very well telling herself that she hated Declan, hated his arrogance and superiority over her, that she didn't care whether or not he came back safely. But deep inside her she was almost sick with anxiety and the last thing she needed was Clare's mocking insinuations.

'I think we'll just disregard that piece of the message, Consuelo,' she said at last.

Consuelo nodded, well pleased. '*Sim, senhorita.* You and I—we manage, *sim*?' She patted the girl's hand. 'And now you let Consuelo dress your shoulder again.'

It was a long, uncomfortable week, and not even the news that Alexandra's father was making satisfactory progress served to lighten her mood. She spent the time pacing about the garden, or playing with the dogs, or helping Consuelo in the kitchen, unable to sit at anything which gave her mind time to think.

Clare did come up a couple of times, uninvited, ostensibly to keep her company, although Alexandra had the feeling that it was Clare who needed someone to talk to. Her husband seemed absorbed in his work and was often away, and she was bound to feel lonely. She spent most of the time describing the life she used to have in São Paulo when her father was employed at the Consulate there, and how often she had seen Declan in those days. Alexandra despised herself for listening to her, but she couldn't help it. She was morbidly interested in anything to do with him.

Five days after Declan's departure, she had an unexpected visitor. She was sitting on the verandah one morning writing a long-delayed letter to Aunt Liz when the dogs set up their usual barking at the approach of an intruder. Consuelo came bustling out to attend to them, disappearing along the path which led to the gate on to the vine bridge. Alexandra frowned curiously, diverted from her task, and soon Consuelo returned, smiling goodhumouredly. Behind her came a stockily built man of medium height, young and attractive, and clearly European.

'Ay, ay, *senhorita*,' called Consuelo cheerfully. 'Is someone to visit.'

Alexandra got to her feet, hastily brushing down the hem of her short skirt. The stranger was regarding her with evident interest and there was something vaguely familiar about the smile that curved his full lips. He mounted the verandah steps behind Consuelo, and she said: 'Is—how you say?—*primo de* Senhor Declan, *senhorita*.'

'His cousin,' put in the man in faultless English, and Alexandra realised why she had thought there was something familiar about him. In appearance he was not a lot like Declan, but the resemblance was there if one looked close enough. 'Enrico Rubiero, *ao seu dispor, senhorita*.'

'How do you do?' Alexandra gave him a shy smile. 'But

124

I'm afraid—Declan is not here.'

'Consuelo tells me so, *senhorita*. And you are the daughter of Professor Tempest who was staying with my cousin some weeks ago, *sim*?'

'That's right. I'm Alexandra Tempest.' She linked her fingers together and looked hopefully towards Consuelo. 'Er —we don't know when Declan will be back, do we, Consuelo?'

'*Nao, senhorita*. Is most unfortunate.'

'My cousin takes his work very seriously,' murmured Enrico dryly.

'His work is serious,' declared Alexandra, unable to prevent the defensive retort, and Enrico raised knowing eyebrows.

'Of course.' He glanced at Consuelo. 'Come,' he said. 'Are you not going to offer me some of your most excellent coffee, *meu velha*?'

Consuelo responded to his flattery with a chuckle. 'Of course, *senhor*. You will stay to lunch?'

Enrico looked towards Alexandra. 'If Senhorita Tempest will permit me,' he agreed.

Alexandra shrugged. 'Oh, of course.' She glanced round. 'Won't you sit down?'

'*Obrigado, senhorita*.'

Enrico took the cane chair beside hers and Consuelo left them to prepare the coffee. After she had gone Alexandra folded her writing pad and put the top on her pen. Enrico was watching her questioningly and she realised it was up to her to make some conversation. But she didn't know what to say !

At last, he said : 'I have interrupted you, *senhorita*. You were writing to your father, perhaps?'

'No. No, to my aunt, actually. As a matter of fact my father doesn't know I'm here.'

'No?' Enrico looked surprised. 'But did you not inform

125

him of your imminent arrival?'

'I'm afraid not.' Alexandra fidgeted with her pen. 'I—I wanted to surprise him, you see, and then when I got here I discovered he was in hospital in Bogota.'

'I see. How unfortunate!' His eyes narrowed. 'And my cousin permitted you to stay with him until your father's return?'

'That's right.'

'It was—most fortunate that Declan was here, was it not?'

'Most fortunate.' Alexandra forced a smile. 'He—he has been very kind.' She put down her pen. 'And you, *senhor*? What brings you to Paradiablo? You do not live here?'

'Oh, no.' Enrico shook his head. 'My home is in São Paulo, *senhorita*. But I have business matters to discuss with my cousin. You understand it is not always easy to get in touch with him.'

Alexandra nodded. 'He is remote.'

'In more ways than one, *senhorita*,' remarked Enrico dryly. 'Ah, here is Consuelo with our coffee. Hmm, it smells *delicioso*!'

When Consuelo had departed again and the coffee was poured, Enrico asked her about her life in England. 'You have a career, *senhorita*?' he suggested, adding sugar to his cup.

Alexandra shook her head. 'I'm still at school, *senhor*.'

'At school?' Enrico was evidently surprised. 'But you do not behave like a schoolgirl, *senhorita*.'

'Thank you,' Alexandra smiled. 'I'll take that as a compliment. Actually, I shall be leaving school in four months. My father expects me to go on to university, but I don't want to.'

'University? Ah, yes. My father wished this for me also. But fortunately there was a family business for me to enter, and this is what I did. I have not regretted it. Are you not

126

interested in bugs, *senhorita*?'

'Bugs?' Alexandra was confused.

'But yes. Is not your father interested in such things?'

'Oh, I see. Well, yes, I suppose he is. But no, I'm no good at biology—any of the sciences.'

Enrico nodded. 'I do not blame you. Such work is not becoming to a woman. Myself, I could not show enthusiam for disease in any form.'

'I don't think anyone is enthusiastic about disease, *senhor*.'

'No, of course not.' Enrico spread his hands. 'I express myself poorly. What I mean to say is—I could not do a job such as your father does. Or Declan either, for that matter.'

'But surely you must agree that someone has to do this work?'

'Y-e-s.' Enrico looked down at his immaculately manicured fingernails. 'But I could not go to these Indian villages as Declan does. I could not treat their diseases, minister to them!' There was distaste in the way he said it. 'Could you, *senhorita*?'

Alexandra hesitated, remembering almost shamefully her own distaste several days ago when the women at the Indian village had tried to be friendly with her. 'I—I don't know.'

'It is easier for some than for others,' he remarked complacently. 'And naturally Declan finds it easier than most.'

Alexandra caught his eyes on her, and she didn't altogether care for their speculative gleam. She realised that he expected her to ask why. But she knew, or at least she thought she did. He was referring to Declan's Indian ancestry.

Changing the subject entirely, she said: 'Did you come up to Paradiablo by air?'

Enrico did not immediately reply, but at last he said: 'Yes, indeed. How else?'

Alexandra nodded, raising her coffee cup to her lips. 'It's a very narrow air-strip, isn't it?'

'I suppose so.' Enrico didn't seem too happy about this turn of the conversation. 'An experienced pilot can negotiate it without difficulty.'

'Do you fly, *senhor*?'

'Not personally, no.' He drew a deep breath. 'Tell me, *senhorita*, has Declan taken you to see the old prospecting site yet?'

Alexandra's nails curled into her palms. 'No. No, he hasn't. He hasn't actually had the time.'

'Of course not.' Enrico was suave. 'His work, I know. And now this outbreak of yellow fever.'

'You know about that?'

'I was informed at the airport that my cousin had sent for further supplies of vaccine, *senhorita*.'

'Oh, I see.' Alexandra put down her cup. 'Would you like some more coffee?'

'*Obrigado, senhorita*.' He pushed his cup towards her. 'And are you not finding it rather lonely here in this isolated outpost?'

'I—not lonely, no.' Alexandra suspected he would like her to express dissatisfaction with the situation, although why she suspected this she could not have said. 'There's Consuelo—oh, and Mrs. Forman. Do you know her, *senhor*?'

'Clare? But of course.' Enrico smiled his thanks for the second cup of coffee. 'I had forgotten her. I expect she is glad of your companionship, too.'

Alexandra smiled. She could not honestly have said that she and Clare shared a companionship either.

'I expect she has told you that she used to live in Sao Paulo, *senhorita*?' Enrico nodded at Alexandra's reluctant affirmation. 'She and my cousin were—great friends.'

'Were they?' Alexandra drained her cup and poured herself another. 'Are you married, *senhor*?'

'Me?' Enrico seemed surprised. 'Not yet, *senhorita*.' He sighed. 'My mother despairs of me. But I enjoy my freedom. As you do, *senhorita*.'

Alexandra looked down into her empty cup. She wished that Consuelo would come back and then she could excuse herself and go to her room. She didn't care for this question and answer session. She decided she didn't altogether care for Enrico Rubiero either.

Much to her relief, Consuelo did put in an appearance a few minutes later. She had come to take away the tray and while Enrico was practising his charm on her, complimenting her on the coffee and asking her what delights she had in store for lunch, Alexandra slipped away to her room. It was a relief to flop down on her bed and relax completely. She supposed she ought to feel grateful that for a few minutes at least Enrico's presence had banished her anxieties about Declan, but his attitude was too much like Clare's for her to feel comfortable with him.

At lunch she was relieved to find that he seemed to have exhausted his questions and instead they talked about general things like art and literature in which Alexandra was quite well versed. She had always enjoyed reading and it was interesting to discover that there were Brazilian authors following the styles of Hemingway and Scott Fitzgerald.

Towards the end of the meal, she said: 'Will you be flying back to São Paulo tonight, *senhor*?'

Enrico reached for a luscious peach and began to peel it. 'I do not know, *senhorita*. Actually, I have been discussing this with Consuelo in your absence, and she has suggested that I might stay until Declan's return.'

Alexandra felt a rising surge of indignation. How dared Consuelo suggest such a thing without first discussing it with her?

'I see.'

Enrico was perceptive. 'I have offended you, *senhorita*?'

Alexandra sighed. 'No, not offended, *senhor*. But surely you realise that while your cousin is away, neither Consuelo nor I can offer his hospitality to anyone without his permission.'

'I am his cousin, *senhorita*,' Enrico pointed out.

'I know that, but...' She moved her shoulders helplessly. 'We don't even know when Declan will return.'

'I am sure it will not be long, *senhorita*. I will send a message to him.'

Alexandra felt as though he had driven her into a corner. 'Very well, *senhor*.'

'Oh, come!' Enrico was contrite. 'Naturally, I will not stay if you do not wish me to do so.'

'*Enrico!*' Clare's surprised exclamation interrupted their conversation, and Alexandra looked up in dismay as the other girl walked into the room. 'Enrico, you dog, why didn't you let us know you were here?'

Enrico rose to his feet, smiling disarmingly. 'Clare! How good it is to see you again.' They embraced, kissing one another on either cheek in the continental fashion. 'And I have not yet had time to do anything, my dear. I arrived only this morning.'

Clare flicked Alexandra an impatient look. 'Hello, Alex,' she observed coolly. 'I hope you've been looking after your guest.'

Alexandra hid her annoyance. 'Won't you join us, Mrs Forman?' she requested, pushing a chair forward. 'We were just having coffee. Perhaps you'd like some.'

'I would.' Clare sat down and crossed her legs elegantly. 'Well, Enrico, and what brings you to this neck of the woods?'

'Business, *naturalmente*.' He gave a mocking smile. 'Surely you did not imagine I had come for my health.'

Clare laughed. 'Who would?' Then she cast a malicious

glance in Alexandra's direction. 'Unless one was absolutely desperate for excitement!'

Alexandra refused to rise to the bait and after a few moments Clare returned her attention to the man. 'Did you know there's an outbreak of yellow fever at Maracuja?'

'Yes. Gruvas told me when I landed. Declan must have his hands full.'

Clare wrinkled her nose. 'Filthy disease! I don't know how he can stand it. Those ghastly huts—no sanitation—the *smell*!'

'Funnily enough, Senhorita Tempest and I were discussing that earlier on, were we not, *senhorita*?' Enrico licked his full lips. 'A man needs dedication, wouldn't you say?'

Clare frowned. 'Declan is dedicated,' she replied. 'Why else would he give up the opportunity of a consultancy at the hospital in São Paulo?'

'Perhaps he feels more at home here,' suggested Enrico slyly, but Alexandra could not let him get away with it.

'It's more likely that he feels that these people need him more than the people of Sao Paulo,' she exclaimed angrily. 'Doctors are not so thick on the ground in Paradiablo!'

'You could be right.' For once Clare agreed with her.

Enrico's lips drew in. 'Always the *senhoritas* defend my so-handsome cousin,' he remarked dryly. 'I have heard that women are attracted by the blood of a primitive!'

'Don't be sarcastic, Enrico,' advised Clare, accepting the coffee Alexandra offered her. 'It's not becoming.' She took a sip from her cup. 'Or I'll begin to think that you're jealous!'

Her eyes challenged his, but Alexandra had had enough. 'If you'll excuse me, I'll clear these things,' she began, and Clare made no demur.

Consuelo was in the kitchen and looked up in surprise when Alexandra came in with a pile of dishes. 'Ay, ay, this is not necessary, *senhorita*!'

131

'I know that, but I wanted to speak to you, Consuelo. Did you invite Senhor Rubiero to stay until Senhor Declan returns?'

Consuelo wrung her hands unhappily. 'Not exactly, *senhorita*.'

'But you did suggest it?'

'*Nao, senhorita*. Senhor Enrico suggest it and Consuelo say—perhaps!'

'I see.' Alexandra sighed. 'Well, I don't see how I can refuse. Do we have room? I mean, without using Senhor Declan's room?'

'*Sim, senhorita*. Is four bedrooms and Consuelo's room.'

'All right. You'd better prepare one of those then.'

'*Sim, senhorita*.' Consuelo chewed anxiously at her lower lip. 'The *senhorita* is not angry with Consuelo?'

Alexandra smiled ruefully. 'I suppose not. By the way, Mrs. Forman is here at the moment and I'm going to ask her and her husband to join us for dinner this evening. I'd rather not spend the evening alone with our guest.'

Consuelo looked worried. 'You do not like him, *senhorita*?'

'Let's say I neither like nor dislike him, shall we?' Alexandra shrugged. 'Oh, and by the way, send a note to Maracuja informing Declan of his cousin's arrival, will you? It —it may bring him home a day or two sooner.'

Consuelo nodded sympathetically. 'You worry about Senhor Declan, do you not, *senhorita*?'

'A little, perhaps.' Alexandra was abrupt. She had no intention of discussing her personal feelings with Consuelo.

'Is no need.' Consuelo spread her hands. 'Senhor Declan is big, strong man! He not get yellow fever.'

Alexandra forced a smile. 'I don't suppose he will. I—I must go back now. You—you won't forget what I asked.'

'No, *senhorita*. I send Paulo at once.'

'Thank you.'

Alexandra returned to the living room, but that fragmentary reference to Declan had disrupted her confidence and she found it incredibly difficult to behave as though nothing had happened. However, Clare was more than willing to accept her dinner invitation, and the ensuing discussion of the merits of Consuelo's cooking enabled her to say little and regain her self-possession.

The evening was, she supposed, a qualified success. Clare obviously found Enrico more engaging than her husband, and Alexandra and David were left to entertain themselves. Not that David seemed to mind. He was a quiet, undemanding sort of man, not at all the kind of man Alexandra would have expected someone like Clare to marry, but he seemed to love his wife and perhaps he was blind to her imperfections.

All the same, Alexandra was inordinately glad when the evening was over and she could retire to her room. She was curiously restless and tearful, and wondered why she should resent so badly the fact that Enrico Rubiero was sleeping here in comfort while Declan might be exposed to all manner of dangers.

She lay wakeful, staring towards the glimmer of moonlight that filtered through the shutters. What was Declan doing at this moment? Was he attending to a patient, or was he sleeping? She rolled on to her stomach, pressing her knuckles against her lips. Did he find Indian women attractive? And were there perhaps Portuguese families living in the village? With dark-eyed, olive-skinned Portuguese daughters?

A sudden sound broke the stillness and she thrust herself up on to her knees, her brows drawn tightly together. What was that? She listened intently. Why weren't the dogs barking?

She sighed, relaxing a little. It was probably one of the dogs who had made the noise in the first place. It couldn't

133

be anything else or they would have soon woken the household. Three nights ago, a roaming mountain lion had passed within hearing distance of the house and its weird screaming roar had sent the dogs almost wild with excitement. Alexandra had been terrified until she was reassured by the knowledge that that must have been one of the reasons why Tom O'Rourke had enclosed the building within a stout wooden barracade.

She was about to lie down again when the distinct sound of something falling in the living room arrested her. Her nerves tautened. Someone was about. Had an intruder managed to evade being overheard after all? She drew a trembling breath. It was no good—she would have to investigate. If it happened to be Enrico Rubiero looking for something she hoped she would be able to escape without being observed.

She slid off the bed, pushed her feet into heelless slippers and reached for the silk dressing gown draped over the end of the bed. She fastened the cord tightly around her slim waist and padded to the door. Consuelo always left a lamp burning dimly in the hall, and the shadows it cast were elongated and unreal.

She went swiftly along the hall before her courage gave out on her. There was a light below the living room door and she halted uncertainly. Surely no intruder would light a lamp, and yet how else could he see what he was doing?

Her fingers closed round the handle and she turned it slowly. The door gave inwards without a sound, and with trembling fingers she pushed it wide enough to get her head round. But the room was deserted. A lamp was burning on the low table by the hearth where the ashes of the dying logs still glimmered, and Declan's box of cigars was lying on the rug beneath the table, its contents scattered, evidence of the sound she had heard earlier. She pushed the door wider and entered the room, a puzzled expression on her face. Someone had been in here quite recently, but where was that someone now? And who was it?

She moved automatically towards the strewn cigars and bent and began picking them up almost without thinking.

'Why aren't you in bed?'

The unexpectedly harsh male tones nearly startled her out of her wits. She dropped the cigars and got unsteadily to her feet.

'*Declan!*' she breathed. 'I—so it was you I heard!'

'I imagine so.' Declan came into the room and kicked the door to behind him. He was carrying a plate in one hand on which reposed a thick, unappetising meat sandwich, and in the other he carried a can of beer. He walked towards the couch and flung himself down wearily. 'You'll have to excuse me if I don't stand on ceremony, but I am rather tired.'

Now that the lamplight was illuminating his face Alexandra could see exactly how weary he looked. Lines of fatigue etched his eyes and mouth, and a kind of grey pallor had entered his cheeks. His hair was rough and unkempt, and he didn't look as if he had changed the denim shirt and pants he was wearing since he left almost six days ago.

She hovered uncertainly at the side of the couch. 'Is—is there anything I can get you?' she asked awkwardly. 'Something else to eat? Another drink?'

He shook his head, resting it back against the cool leather upholstery. 'Nothing,' he said, swallowing a mouthful of the beer. 'Go to bed!'

Alexandra sighed. 'Was—was it very bad?' she ventured.

He lifted his head and turned exhausted eyes in her direction. 'What do you think?'

She shook her head, looking down at her fingers playing with the cord of her dressing gown. 'Did—did you get my message?'

'Of course.' He rested his head back again.

135

Alexandra still hesitated. She was loath to leave him. She had the feeling that if she did he would simply fall asleep there on the couch and awake feeling stiff and un-rested in the morning. She turned back to the cigars and began picking them up again.

'For God's sake, Alexandra,' he muttered, turning to look at her, 'Go to bed! I'm sorry if I disturbed you, but my reflexes are not as alert as they usually are.'

'I wasn't asleep,' she replied, putting the rest of the cig-ars into the box and standing it down on the table in front of him. 'I—I was thinking about you, actually.'

'Were you?' He sounded uninterested.

'Yes.' She paused. 'I was wondering how you were get-ting on. Is the epidemic under control now?'

Declan heaved a sigh. 'Do you mind if we have this con-versation in the morning? I'm not really in the mood for small talk.'

Still she lingered. She watched him finish his sandwich and wash it down with the last of his beer. Then he thrust the plate and can aside and closed his eyes. She guessed he was half asleep already.

'Declan?'

'Hmm?'

'Declan, won't you go to your room? I mean, you can't sleep here!'

His eyes flickered open. 'Why not?'

'Well, because—because you'll be uncomfortable——'

'Uncomfortable?' He shook his head irritably. 'Alex-andra, are you aware that for the past week such sleep as I have had has been in a hammock, strung up like a monkey! This couch is a feather bed compared to that!'

Alexandra twisted her hands together. 'Maybe so. But you're here now, and it seems a pity——'

'All right!' He made a gesture as if he was pushing away her unwelcome attentions. 'All right, I'll go to my room, if that will persuade you to go to yours!'

Alexandra stepped back a pace and he got to his feet, reaching for the lamp. But he swayed and the lamp would have overturned had she not caught it in time.

'God, I must be more tired than I thought,' he muttered grimly. 'I'm sorry. I'm all right now. Give me the lamp!'

'I'll put it in your room,' she said firmly, and walked ahead of him out of the door.

She put the lamp on the chest of drawers in his room, well away from the bed, just in case he should reach out and knock it over during the night. Declan came unsteadily into the room and dropped down on to his bed wearily, resting his head in his hands. Then, as though becoming conscious of her scrutiny, he lifted bloodshot eyes to her face.

'Well?' he asked resignedly, 'what are you waiting for?'

Alexandra shook her head. 'Nothing.'

'Then go to your room,' he adjured impatiently. 'I'll be all right. All I need is sleep.'

He stretched out on the bed and closed his eyes, and unable to find any reasonable reason for remaining she went back to her room. But not to sleep.

She paced about restlessly, conscious that he had not even taken off his boots and that his face and body were grimed with sweat. In the normal way he would never have gone to sleep like that.

Eventually, after about half an hour, she tiptoed back to his room again, going inside quietly and closing the door. He had not moved, as she had expected, and she stood looking at him with a curiously protective pain stirring inside her stomach. In sleep he looked younger, more vulnerable, and infinitely attractive.

Biting her lip, she approached the bed and lifted one of his feet. His boot came off without difficulty, and he didn't stir. Emboldened by her success, she pulled off the other boot and his socks as well. Then she paused. He was in a deep slumber, and she doubted that anything would wake him, but sponging his face and chest would require some courage.

Kneeling down beside him, she unfastened the remaining buttons of his shirt and unbuckled the belt of his trousers. The shirt pulled away quite easily and it wasn't difficult to slide it off his shoulders by rolling him on to his side. She breathed more freely when the shirt had been tossed aside for washing. Apart from a protesting grunt he had made no sound and she hurried into the bathroom and came back with a warm soapy sponge and a towel.

She sponged his body first, using firm strokes that did not seem to disturb him. Then she lowered him back against the pillows and went to rinse the sponge before tackling his face. His skin looked clean and infinitely fresher, and she gained confidence from her success. She was drying his face with the towel when his eyes flickered open and he stared at her for a moment without recognition.

She bumped back against her heels, her hands trembling, hoping against hope that he would close his eyes again. But he didn't. He ran a questing hand over his bare chest and then, encountering the unfastened belt of his trousers, he jack-knifed into a sitting position.

'What the hell do you think you're doing?' he demanded roughly.

Alexandra would have scrambled to her feet and backed away, but his hand shot out and captured her upper arm, wrenching her towards him. 'I asked what you thought you were doing?' he said between his teeth.

'Oh, Declan, I was just freshening you up,' she exclaimed painfully. 'Will you let go of my arm? You're hurting me!'

'And was it part of your plan to undress me, too?' he enquired grimly, snatching the towel out of her hands and

138

throwing it aside.

'*No!*' Alexandra was appealing. 'Declan, I only wanted to help you——'

'To help me? Oh, *God*!' He released her abruptly and fell back against the pillows, closing his eyes.

'What's the matter?' Alexandra didn't move away but stared down anxiously at him. 'Are you ill?'

His eyes opened. 'No, Alexandra, I'm not ill. I'm tired, that's all.' He groaned wearily. 'Look—all right, I appreciate your motives were of the best, but I don't honestly care whether I'm filthy or otherwise. Why don't you just go away like a good girl and leave me to *sleep*?'

Alexandra sniffed miserably. 'I'm sorry.'

'Are you?' He regarded her through the thickness of his lashes. 'Oh, Alexandra, stop looking so hurt! I know I'm an ungrateful swine, but honestly, I really am exhausted.'

'I know.' She half turned away. 'I—I'll tell Consuelo not to disturb you in the morning——'

'Just a minute!' He propped himself up on one elbow and reached out a hand towards her. After a moment, she put her hand into his and he drew her towards the bed. 'What's the matter?' he asked gently. 'Can't you sleep?'

Alexandra flushed. 'I was worried about you.'

He studied her wan face for several seconds and then he nodded. 'Yes, I believe you were.' He indicated the lamp on the chest of drawers. 'Go and turn that out for me, would you?'

Sighing, she went and did as he had asked, waiting for a moment as her eyes accustomed themselves to the gloom before making for the door. As she passed the bed, she was conscious of his eyes upon her, and then he murmured: 'Don't go, Alexandra. Stay with me!'

Her heart was pounding so loudly that she had difficulty in believing what she had heard. 'I—what did you say?' she stammered.

He leant across and caught the folds of her gown. 'You heard me,' he replied quietly. 'Don't be alarmed. It's a purely innocent offer. I'm too tired to be of any danger to you. But you're welcome to share my bed if it might help you to sleep.'

Alexandra caught her breath. 'But—I couldn't!'

'Why not? We've slept together before.'

'I know, but that was different.'

'How was it different?'

'Well——' She sought for words. 'I can't just *sleep* with you!'

'Why not?' He was beginning to sound impatient. 'Alexandra, where is the harm in two people sharing the same bed? Here, it happens all the time.'

Alexandra hesitated. She wanted to stay. But her reasons for staying and his for asking her were vastly different things.

'If—if Consuelo——'

'Leave Consuelo to me,' he remarked dryly, pulling her towards the bed, and she let him.

It was marvellously comforting to feel his warm body next to hers, even though he did turn away from her, and when she heard his breathing become slow and regular, she nestled into the small of his back and slipped one arm around his waist.

CHAPTER NINE

ALEXANDRA was up in the morning long before Declan was awake. She awoke just after seven-thirty to find Declan's arm enclosing her waist, and his face buried in the silken swathe of her hair. She was loath to move and possibly risk disturbing him, but the scarcity of attire afforded by the thin silken gown was sufficient to persuade her that she ought to make the effort now, while she could.

In fact, he didn't even stir, and she stood for several minutes just looking at him, wondering how she had lived almost eighteen years of her life without knowing of his existence. In such a short space of time he had become the most important being in her world, and it was a terrifying thought, particularly as he still considered her a child.

Shaking away the feelings of despondency which threatened to overwhelm her, she opened the door as quietly as she could and stepped out into the hall. She walked along to her bedroom and then halted aghast. Consuelo was in her room, making her bed, and she smiled knowingly when she looked up and saw Alexandra.

'*Bom dia, senhorita,*' she greeted her cheerfully. 'You slept well, *sim*?'

Alexandra's cheeks burned. She couldn't help it. 'I— what are you doing in here, Consuelo?' she asked, trying to appear calm.

'Your door was open, *senhorita*. Consuelo is making your bed, is all. Is no good?'

Alexandra shook her head impatiently. 'It doesn't matter.' She moved into the room. 'Er—Senhor Declan came back last night.'

'*Sim, senhorita*, I know.'

'You *know*?'

'*Sim, senhorita*. Consuelo hear you—together.'

If anything, Alexandra felt even worse. 'You—heard us?'

'Is no matter, *senhorita*. Consuelo get up to make sure Senhor Declan is all right. She hear you talking.'

'Oh! Oh, I see.' Alexandra breathed again. 'Well, he—he was very tired. I—I looked in on him just now, to make sure he was still asleep. He asked me to ask you not to wake him this morning.'

Consuelo smoothed the coverlet and straightened. '*Sim, senhorita*,' she agreed politely, and Alexandra couldn't decide what she meant by it.

'Is Senhor Rubiero up yet?'

Consuelo shook her head. '*Nao, senhorita*. But he does not know that Senhor Declan is back.'

'No, no, he wouldn't.' Alexandra bit her lip. 'I'll get dressed.'

'*Sim, senhorita*.' Consuelo moved towards the door and then she paused. 'Is a good man, Senhor Declan, *senhorita*. An honourable man!'

Alexandra's lips parted. 'I—I'm sure he is.'

'He would not hurt you, *senhorita*.'

Alexandra didn't know how to answer her. She moved her shoulders helplessly and smiled.

'Consuelo think the *senhorita* is fond of Senhor Declan.' The old housekeeper was not to be diverted.

Alexandra sighed. 'He's been very—kind.'

Consuelo nodded vigorously. 'Is a kind man.'

'I know that.' Alexandra didn't quite know what this was leading up to, but she sensed Consuelo's desire to arouse her sympathy. She wondered why. Did Consuelo know what had happened last night? Did she imagine that because of it Declan had made love to her? Her heart fluttered a little at the thought. Was this Consuelo's way of excusing what she imagined he had done? 'You don't have to extol Declan's virtues to me, Consuelo,' she added. 'I'm quite aware that without his help I'd have been in real trouble.'

Consuelo stared at her intently. 'Is so?'

'Of course.' Alexandra turned away. 'I'll have breakfast in fifteen minutes, Consuelo, if that's all right.'

Consuelo hesitated only a moment longer and then with a shrug she went out of the door. Alexandra waited until the door of the kitchen had opened and closed behind her before closing her own door, and then she leant back against it weakly. What a situation! She had no idea whether Consuelo knew she had slept in Declan's room or otherwise, and she wondered what he would say if the housekeeper spoke so ambiguously to him.

Enrico Rubiero appeared as she was enjoying her first cup of coffee and approached the table, stretching lazily.

'Hmm, the mornings here are quite something, are they not?' he offered as a greeting. 'And might I say how charming you look, *senhorita*?'

'Thank you.' Alexandra forced a polite smile.

He paused and looked across the verandah to the heavily-perfumed flamboyance of the garden. 'Yes. I am beginning to see that there are compensations for living here.'

Alexandra busied herself pouring a second cup of coffee. 'Did you know that Declan is back, *senhor*?'

'Declan? Back already?' Enrico looked surprised. 'No, I did not. That was sudden, was it not?'

'I—I believe Consuelo sent a message.' Alexandra flicked an insect from the polished surface of the table. 'He must have felt able to leave or he would not have done so.'

Enrico frowned and seated himself opposite her. 'Indeed.' He tapped his fingers impatiently. 'And you, *senhorita*? How much longer do you expect to remain here?'

'I'm not sure. Until my father returns from hospital, I suppose.'

'And what makes you think your father will return here, *senhorita*? Surely, if he has been ill, it would be more natural for him to return to England.'

Alexandra felt the first twinges of doubt. 'I haven't really thought about it,' she confessed. 'I—I expect I thought he would want to complete his survey.'

Enrico drew a deep breath. 'He has had blood poisoning, has he not? Clare spoke of this last night. I think it would be most unwise for him to return here. He will be weak. He will need to—how do you say it?—recuperate?'

Alexandra pushed her cup aside. 'Then I shall just have to wait and see what happens, shan't I, *senhor*?'

Enrico raised his dark eyebrows. 'Perhaps my cousin has reasons of his own for keeping you here, *senhorita*. I should take care. Declan has quite a reputation with the ladies. Ask Clare!'

Alexandra got to her feet. She had no intention of asking Clare anything. 'I'll tell Consuelo you're here, *senhor*,' she said, and with a faint inclination of her head she walked away.

But it was not so easy to dismiss what he had intimated, she found. There had been some truth in what he had suggested, and it was quite possible that her father, unaware of her presence at Paradiablo, might conceivably decide to fly home for a few weeks before resuming his studies. He would expect her to be in Cannes, with Aunt Liz, and what better place for a few weeks' recuperation?

Distinctly out of humour with herself, she went to the kitchen, told Consuelo that their guest was waiting for his breakfast, and then left the house by the rear door.

144

The dogs were loose and came bounding to meet her. She had grown quite accustomed to them during these past days and she fondled their heads warmly, finding their undemanding friendship a welcome relief from so much intrigue.

She was still playing with them when the man who was occupying so much of her thoughts came strolling round the side of the building. He looked much different this morning from the haggard-eyed individual of the night before, his hair damp from the shower, his clothes fitting his lean body closely. Only his shirt was unfastened, revealing the hair-roughened strength of his torso.

'Good morning,' he greeted her lazily, and she quickly threw away the ball she was holding so that both dogs bounded after it.

'Good morning.' The colour rose into her face. 'How do you feel this morning?'

'Much better,' he commented, sliding his thumbs into the low belt of his trousers. 'How about you?'

Alexandra shrugged. 'I'm okay.' She glanced back towards the house. 'Have you seen your cousin?'

'Enrico? Briefly. He has some papers for me to sign. I believe he's getting them ready.' The dogs came bounding back, this time making for Declan, their tongues hanging out with the heat. He bent and made a fuss of them, grinning as they almost overbalanced him. 'What are you doing out here?'

She moved awkwardly. 'Nothing much. I enjoy playing with the dogs. They're good company.'

He straightened. 'And have you found the days dragging since I left?'

'Some.' She lifted her shoulders and let them fall. 'I—is everything under control at Maracuja?'

He frowned. 'The sisters from the convent at Vareja are coping. I'll go back, perhaps tomorrow.'

'You're going back!' She couldn't keep the dismay out of her voice.

'I must. It will not be for much longer.'

Disappointment brought a sulky twist to her mouth. 'Then why did you come?' she demanded. 'Why didn't you wait that little bit longer?'

Declan's expression hardened. 'And leave you here with Enrico for company, is that what you mean?'

That was not at all what she meant, but Alexandra refused to let him have it all his own way. 'Why not?' she asked provocatively.

Declan folded his arms. 'I prefer that so long as you remain in my charge you shall not be placed in positions of compromise!'

'What?' Alexandra stared at him disbelievingly. 'I don't know what you're talking about.'

'My cousin is not like me, Alexandra. He might conceivably get the wrong impression of your situation here.'

Alexandra gasped. 'Oh, really? And what if I tell you that he has practically said the same thing about you?'

Declan had a pulse working low on his jawline. 'I do not care what my cousin has said about me, Alexandra. But while you are at Paradiablo, I am responsible for you.'

Alexandra felt bitter. 'Isn't it a bit late to start talking about compromising situations?' she asked mockingly. 'I hardly think you're in a position to judge!'

A deep frown drew his brows together. 'Have a care, Alexandra. You're not speaking to one of your schoolboy admirers now!'

'Are you an admirer, then, Declan?' she taunted, making a face at him. 'I thought I was too young for your tastes.'

He shook his head disgustedly, and half turned away from her. 'I can see I've chosen the wrong moment to speak to you,' he said coldly. 'Let me know when you're prepared to behave sensibly and we'll continue this conversation.'

146

Alexandra instantly regretted her foolishness. 'Declan,' she appealed, as he began to walk away. 'Declan, I'm sorry.' She hunched her shoulders. 'I—I was disappointed, that's all.'

He studied her tremulous young face dispassionately. 'Disappointed?' he echoed. 'Alexandra, you know I have my work to do.'

'I suppose I'm childish, like you say.'

He sighed, walking slowly back to her. 'And lonely, perhaps,' he suggested, touching her cheek almost absently.

'Not when you're here,' she breathed, and heard his swift intake of breath and the word he uttered which did not bear repeating.

'Alexandra, I thought I had made the situation very plain to you——'

'Oh, yes.' She was bitter. 'I know, I know.' She stiffened her slim shoulders. 'What was it you wanted to speak to me about?'

He shook his head impatiently, putting an arm around her shoulders and drawing her close to his side. 'You really are a menace, do you know that?' he muttered huskily against her hair. 'And this kind of thing is madness!'

'Why? Why is it?' She raised her face to his and saw the unmistakable darkening of passion in his eyes.

'Your father wouldn't approve,' he said, stroking her face with his free hand.

'How can you say that?'

Declan's eyes dropped the slender length of her and returned to rest almost tangibly on her mouth. 'I just know it,' he pronounced quietly. 'Your father is very proud of you. He expects great things of you, I'm sure.'

'How do you *know*?'

'He talked a lot about you when he was here. I got to feel I knew you already. That was why—well, when I found that you were at Los Hermanos, I had to come and fetch

147

you. For his sake.'

'And what did he tell you? Did you approve?'

'*Alexandra!*' He spoke through his teeth.

'Well, did you?'

Declan narrowed his eyes and his hand slid down her neck to cup one rounded breast. 'I'm twelve years older than you, Alexandra,' he groaned, in a hoarse voice.

'What has age got to do with it?' She pressed herself against him. 'You want to make love to me, don't you?'

Declan gave a muffled ejaculation and then he covered her mouth with his own, gathering her closer to him until she could feel the throbbing hardness of his desire.

'I seem to be interrupting something, don't I?'

Clare's malicious words separated them as successfully as a douche of cold water might have done. Declan thrust Alexandra almost roughly away from him and wiped his mouth deliberately with the back of his hand.

'No, Clare,' he denied, with an element of relief in his voice. 'You're not interrupting anything.'

Alexandra stared at him. That he should stand there and deny his own involvement after what had just occurred. How despicable! Without saying a word to either of them she turned and marched away towards the house.

In her room she paced miserably back and forth. She was trying not to give in to the tears that burned the back of her eyes and added their own discomfort to the despair she was already experiencing. How could Declan behave as if she were some precocious teenager he was having to contend with? He had practically welcomed Clare's appearance as an escape from her unwanted attentions. How could he? *How could he?* He had been aroused. She had had physical evidence of it.

She pressed her palms to her hot cheeks. It might have been better if Declan had not shown any tenderness towards her, but she could not believe that he was an unwilling

148

participant on every occasion.

She drew a trembling breath. Well, there was only one thing to do so long as she remained in this house, and that was to avoid him on every occasion. She would speak when necessary, be polite when spoken to, but until her father's return she would not be made a fool of again.

Pondering her father's return as a welcome relief from the torture of more intimate thoughts, she began to wonder whether she wouldn't be more sensible to return to São Paulo when Enrico Rubiero left and make her way home to England from there. Either that or insist on being flown to Bogota. Perhaps Declan would have fewer objections about taking her to her father now.

But the prospect of leaving Paradiablo, of leaving this house which she had grown to love—and most particularly, of leaving Declan—filled her with desperation. How could she return to England and expect to take up her life as though nothing momentous had happened? How could she consider returning to the friendly camaraderie of co-educational school life when her whole system revolted against such a course?

She was no longer a schoolgirl. These past few weeks she had become a woman. But what point had she for remaining? Declan despised her for revealing her immature feelings so openly; Clare no doubt found the whole affair unutterably amusing; while her father ... She shook her head and walked dispiritedly towards the window. What would her father say if she told him she was in love with a man whose home was in the foothills of the upper Amazon basin? A man who seemed to have no desire to live in the accepted pattern? She could answer her own question. He would be horrified. And he, with his lack of understanding of emotional feelings, would never condone their relationship. In that at least Declan had been right, although his motives for saying so and hers were on vastly different levels. It was an impossible situation, and the sooner it was resolved the better.

She glanced at her watch. It was after one o'clock. She wondered if Clare had been invited to stay for lunch. No doubt she would enjoy having the company of two attractive men.

A light tap at her door brought a stiffening to her body. 'Who—who is it?'

'Consuelo, *senhorita*. May I come?'

'Yes. Come in.' Alexandra's tone was resigned, and she composed herself as the door opened and the housekeeper appeared.

'Is lunch, *senhorita*. You come, please?'

Alexandra hesitated. 'Is—is Senhora Forman still here?'

'*Sim, senhorita*.' Consuelo's lips thinned sympathetically. 'Is no good?'

Alexandra sighed. 'I'm not very hungry, Consuelo. Will you—will you give them my apologies, and I shan't be joining them for lunch.'

Consuelo looked disapproving. 'The *senhorita* is not eating lunch because of the *senhora*!' she declared.

Alexandra shook her head. 'I've told you, Consuelo, I'm not hungry!'

Consuelo patently didn't believe her. 'Consuelo will give your message, *senhorita*,' she said, nodding vigorously. 'And afterwards, I will see you are all right.'

Alexandra didn't quite know what she meant, but she couldn't summon the effort to enquire. So she nodded and thanked her and after the door had closed sank down wearily on to her bed.

She had been sitting there for perhaps half an hour when Consuelo came back, this time carrying a tray.

'I bring your lunch, *senhorita*.' She smiled. 'Is beef. Very good. You like, *sim*?'

Alexandra got up to examine the food on the tray. She

150

could not have offended the old woman by behaving otherwise. And in any case, the skewered curls of beef lying on a bed of flaky rice looked most appetising.

'This is thoughtful of you, Consuelo,' she murmured, moved by the housekeeper's kindness.

'Is nothing,' Consuelo shrugged. 'Is our secret, *sim*?'

After she had gone, Alexandra made an effort to eat something. She was empty, but her throat was so constricted it would only allow her to swallow the smallest morsels. Even so, with the aid of the wine Consuelo had also supplied she managed to eat some of the rice and she lay on her bed afterwards feeeling a little less lost and alone.

She must have slept, because she was startled awake by someone knocking at her door. The skirt of the simple poplin dress she was wearing had ridden up over her hips, and she was smoothing it down as she called: 'Come in!'

She had expected it to be Consuelo, not the angry-looking man whose swift survey of the room took in the congealing beef on the tray and Alexandra's obvious state of *deshabillé*.

'What the hell do you think you're doing, sulking in your room all day?' he demanded harshly. He gestured towards the tray. 'Having Consuelo bring your meals in here, instead of joining us at table. Sending lies about not being hungry!'

Alexandra scrambled off the bed. 'They weren't lies. I wasn't hungry.'

'Then what is the meaning of this?' Again Declan indicated the tray.

'I—Consuelo brought it. She—she felt sorry for me.'

'Sorry for you?' Declan sounded furious. 'Why the hell should she feel sorry for you? What have you been telling her?'

'I haven't told her anything.' Alexandra swallowed convulsively. 'She—she has eyes. She can see.'

'What can she see?'

Alexandra bent her head. 'Oh, does it matter? Please—go away! I don't want to talk to you.'

Declan's answer was to kick the door shut with his foot It slammed with an uncompromising bang.

'I suppose you're behaving this way because of wha' happened this morning?' he suggested coldly.

'Whatever gave you that idea?' Alexandra forced a sar-casm. 'Oh, for heaven's sake! What do you want me tc say? I didn't feel like eating lunch at your table. I had no intention of giving Mrs. Forman further scope for her mali-cious tongue!'

'How did you know Clare was staying for lunch?'

Alexandra coloured. 'I—I guessed.'

'You mean Consuelo told you, don't you?'

'I don't intend to bring Consuelo into this. She's the only person who's shown me any kindness here!'

'Is she?' Declan's face was grim. 'I'd be interested to hear your definition of that word—*kindness*! If you mean she's treated you like a spoilt child, then I'd agree with you.'

Alexandra caught her breath, but she refused to let him see how easily he could hurt her. 'Well, that's what I am, aren't I?' she retorted, controlling her trembling lips with difficulty. 'You're always telling me so. But you needn't worry about me any longer. I'm going to take myself out of your hair!'

'What do you mean?'

'Just what I say. I—I'm leaving!'

'Are you?' Declan's lips thinnned. 'And just how do you propose to accomplish this feat?'

'I—I shall go to São Paulo when Senhor Rubiero leaves. I can easily get a flight from there. I don't mind how many stopovers I have to make.'

152

'Really?' Declan folded his arms. 'And what's brought this on? Our—*contretemps*, earlier?'

'*Contretemps?*' Alexandra gasped. 'I don't enjoy being humiliated in front of Clare Forman!'

'And do you think your life would be any easier if Clare thought there was something between us?' he snapped.

'I—I don't know what you mean——'

'Forget it!' He drew a deep breath. 'So you want to leave with Enrico, do you? Well, I'm afraid that's impossible. He's on his way to the air-strip at this moment.'

'What?' Alexandra stared at him in dismay. 'He can't be!'

'I'm afraid he is. One of my men, Gruvas, arrived from the airport with the car and Enrico decided he might as well leave now as later.'

Alexandra tried to grasp what he was saying. 'Why— why did Gruvas come here? Did you—send for him?'

'No.' He was brusque.

She hesitated, touching her lips with her fingers. 'It—it wasn't to do with my father, was it? Did—did he bring some news?'

Declan tapped long brown fingers against his thigh. 'In a manner of speaking, yes. I had news of your father this morning, but you chose not to listen——'

'What news?' Her eyes were wide and anxious. 'Why didn't you tell me?'

'Calm down,' he advised coldly. 'There's no panic. Your father is much improved.'

'Are you sure?'

He stepped to one side and gestured towards the door. 'Go and see for yourself. It was he, and his assistant, who brought Gruvas from the airport.'

'What?' Alexandra hesitated only long enough to cast a disbelieving glance in Declan's direction before rushing out of the room. The living room door was closed, but she

153

could hear the murmur of voices from beyond. Her courage almost failed her. With a fast-beating heart she reached for the handle, faltering as her fingers encountered the cold steel.

Then Declan's cool voice just behind her said: 'Go ahead! Open it. He won't bite you. He knows you're here.'

'He *knows*?' Alexandra stared at him over her shoulder. 'But—but you said you wouldn't tell him.'

Declan reached past her, his firm fingers closing over hers, forcing her to open the door. 'Don't be a little fool!' he murmured harshly, and with a frown puckering her brow she was propelled forcibly into the room.

Her father was standing on the hearth before the log-piled grate. He was exactly as she remembered him, tall and thin, his greying hair needing cutting and straggling over his opened collar. The lamps had been lit, and the shadows accentuated the hollows in his cheekbones, but apart from a general air of fatigue, due no doubt to the journey, he looked quite well.

But it was the woman standing beside him who focused Alexandra's attention. Clare was not around, and of course, this had to be her father's female assistant. Tall, but generously proportioned, Juana de los Vargos looked about thirty-five, with a coil of coal-black hair and magnolia pale features. She was very attractive, and her sleek green slack suit made Alexandra supremely conscious of the crumpled appearance she must present.

'Alexandra!' Her father's voice was gruff, and with a little cry she ran towards him, surprised at the warmth of his embrace. 'Alex, what in the world possessed you to come here looking for me, child?'

Alexandra's eyes were moist. 'I—I wanted to see you,' she murmured, realising how inadequate that must sound. 'Oh, Father, it is good to see you again. How—how are you?'

Professor Tempest shook his head. 'I'm fully recovered now. Declan no doubt told you all about my little disaster.'

Alexandra gave Declan a swift glance. 'The blood poisoning? Yes, he told me.'

'A most unfortunate occurrence,' agreed her father, nodding. 'Coming as it did at the very end of my research.' Then he looked at the woman at his side. 'Well, not altogether unfortunate,' he amended, with a small smile.

Alexandra looked at Juana de los Vargos now. She was still standing beside them with an air of confidence which Alexandra found vaguely annoying. As though realising that introductions were in order, Professor Tempest drew a deep breath.

'Juana, my dear,' he said, disentangling himself from his daughter and taking the other woman's arm. 'Juana, you'll have gathered that this is my little wayward Alex.' The Colombian woman gave a slight smile, and he went on: 'Alex, my child, I have some rather startling news for you. I intended breaking it when I flew out to Cannes to join you and Elizabeth in a few days, but then I received the letter Elizabeth had sent to the Institute in Rio, and learned that you were here.'

Alexandra's eyes were drawn irresistibly to Declan. So he had not told her father, Aunt Liz had! A feeling of foreboding weakened her knees. She knew what was to come. And she didn't want to hear it!

Her father was patting Juana's arm now, and she was looking confidingly up at him. 'You've no doubt guessed what we have to tell you, Alex,' Professor Tempest continued gently. 'Juana and I were married in Bogota three days ago.'

CHAPTER TEN

It was raining. Huge drops fell heavily on to the flowers, snapping off the petals, bending the stalks. The garden was veiled in a grey curtain of water that saturated the soil and sent up a pungent odour of earth and vegetation and rotting wood. Alexandra stood by the open verandah door, hugging herself closely. She stared out unseeingly, conscious only of the scents from the garden which she felt would always remind her of this devastating period of her life.

She sighed heavily, and suddenly became conscious that someone had entered the room behind her. She swung round on her heels to find Clare Forman shedding a sodden mackintosh, shaking out her umbrella.

Alexandra's nerves tightened. Clare was the last person she needed to see right now. After her father's startling revelations of the night before, and the subsequent discomfort of the supper party that followed, Alexandra felt totally unequipped to deal with someone like Clare Forman.

'I hear you're leaving,' she remarked, by way of a greeting, and Alexandra turned back to her contemplation of the garden.

'Who told you that?'

'Your father. Who else? I saw him yesterday afternoon. Before I left.'

'Oh! Oh, I see.' Alexandra bent her head. 'Did you also meet his—his wife?'

'Juana?' Clare gave a light laugh. 'Of course. I could have told you the way the wind was blowing before they left here.'

Alexandra glanced back at her. 'Do you—know her well?'

'Reasonably.' Clare pulled a pack of cigarettes out of her pocket and lit one. 'She's not the sort of person one ever gets to know really well though. No other woman, that is.'

Alexandra hesitated. 'I—I suppose Declan knew, too.'

'Naturally. They stayed in his home, you know.'

'Umm.' Alexandra stared out at the falling rain. Her eyes felt tight and drawn, due no doubt to the amount of weeping she had done the night before, but at least now she felt drained and not in any danger of making a fool of herself in front of Clare. 'I—I never thought my father would ever marry again.'

Clare flung herself down on to the leather couch. 'That's always the way. Look at me and Declan! He never thought I would marry anyone else either.'

'You—and Declan?' Alexandra turned slowly. 'I don't understand.'

Clare shrugged. 'You know I've told you how—close we were. Surely you guessed we were—lovers?'

Alexandra's stomach twisted. 'I—I never thought about it,' she lied tautly.

Clare looked sceptical, but she ignored the obvious rejoinder and went on: 'Well, Declan and I were virtually engaged when he decided he would like to work at Paradiablo. He asked me to come with him. I refused.'

'You refused?'

Clare sighed impatiently. 'Yes. I was young—and reckless. I couldn't imagine myself living in a place like this.'

'I see.'

'Don't you want to know what happened?'

Alexandra shook her head. 'It's nothing to do with me.'

'Perhaps not. But I'll tell you anyway.' Clare's smile was brittle. 'Declan came up here, and while he was away I

157

married David. When Declan came back for me—I was unattainable.'

Alexandra felt sick. She had suspected something like this all along, and now to have it confirmed ... She turned away, gesturing futilely towards the weather. 'How—how long do you think this is going to last?'

Clare's face hardened. 'You can't fool me, you know, Alex. I know exactly what you're thinking.'

Alexandra tightened the hold she had upon herself. 'What have my thoughts to do with you?'

'Everything. I'm not blind, you know. I have eyes. I've seen the way you look at Declan, the way you try to attract his attention. And yesterday——'

'Oh, really, Clare!'

'No. You listen to me!' Clare got to her feet and came across to her, her face contorted with anger. 'I've told you some of what's between Declan and me, now I'm going to tell you the rest.'

Alexandra shook her head. 'I don't want to hear——'

'No. But you're going to anyway. If only to get rid, once and for all, of those childish little fantasies you've been weaving about you and Declan.'

Alexandra tried to move away, but Clare caught her arm in a compelling grasp, imprisoning her in front of her.

'I realised my mistake,' she said tightly. 'It was always Declan I wanted. That was why when this post came vacant up here, I persuaded David to take it. It meant Declan and I would be near one another. You're not immature enough not to realise what happened!'

'Let—go—of—me!' Alexandra twisted away from her. 'You—you're revolting!'

Clare let her go then, a mocking smile replacing her anger. 'Just so long as you're aware of the facts,' she commented maliciously. 'I'm sorry I had to break it to you so cruelly, but what is it they say about the end justifying the means?'

Alexandra didn't wait to hear any more. She pushed past her and almost ran across the room, colliding full tilt with the man who was just entering.

'Alex, my child!' Her father's face was mildly reproving. 'Can't you look where you're going?'

Alexandra halted reluctantly. 'I—I'm sorry, Father.'

He patted her shoulder. 'That's all right.' He looked beyond his daughter to where Clare was standing. 'Good morning, Mrs. Forman. Rather a change in the weather, isn't there? Lucky for us we arrived yesterday. Couldn't have made it today.'

Clare was composed. She walked back to the couch and sat down. 'Never mind, these storms are soon over. When do you expect to leave?'

'As soon as possible. I want to introduce Juana to my sister,' Professor Tempest smiled. 'Actually, that's what I came to discuss with Alex.'

'Would you rather I left you alone?' Clare moved to the edge of her seat.

'Heavens, no!'

Professor Tempest had no conception of his daughter's frame of mind. But then he never had, thought Alexandra bitterly. He had never tried to understand her, and she doubted that he ever would. That was why his marriage to Juana de los Vargos was so astonishing. She had thought him without the need of any woman.

'I thought we might fly down to Rio tomorrow,' her father was continuing. 'Naturally, I want to visit the Institute, and Juana has friends she wishes to see. No one knows about our marriage, you see.'

Alexandra drew a deep breath. 'Anything you say,' she agreed expressionlessly.

Professor Tempest frowned. 'Doesn't the idea of a few days in Rio appeal to you, Alex? I should have thought you'd have looked forward to seeing the cultural capital of Brazil.'

Alexandra shrugged. 'I could always fly straight back to England. Aunt—Aunt Liz might appreciate my company. Has she been to Cannes?'

'Now you must know she hasn't, Alex. Elizabeth was too concerned about your activities to take herself off for a holiday. I haven't said anything to you so far concerning your complete lack of consideration for your aunt, but there remains a great deal to be explained. How, for instance, did you get the necessary information and inoculations to come out here?'

Alexandra cast a resentful look in Clare's direction. How she would be enjoying this, she thought angrily.

'Can't we discuss it later, Father?' she suggested, with a helpless gesture. 'I—if I'm leaving, I have packing to do.'

Her father clicked his tongue irritably. 'You might go and have a few words with Juana,' he remarked. 'You hardly spoke to her last evening.'

Alexandra scuffed her toe. 'You can't expect Juana and me to have a lot to say to one another yet, Father. We—we hardly know one another.'

'And you never will unless you make an effort,' he retorted. 'Really, Alex, talking about flying back to London alone!'

'I thought this was your honeymoon. I don't want to intrude.'

Her father's mouth drew in. 'I don't recall mentioning any honeymoon, Alex——'

'I think your daughter needs a little time to grow accustomed to the situation, Professor.' Clare's cool tones were faintly amused, and Alexandra's fists clenched. 'After all, Alex is old enough to understand that her position in your household is going to be vastly changed, but not old enough to appreciate that a man needs more out of life than a daughter can give him.'

Professor Tempest turned to Clare with some relief. 'Yes, Mrs. Forman, I'm sure you're right. And perhaps Juana needs a little time, too, to become used to our British reserve.' He smiled. 'When Alexandra returns to school at the end of the summer vac——'

'I'm not returning to school, Father!' Alexandra's clear statement arrested him in full spiel.

'I beg your pardon?'

'I'm not returning to school, Father. I'm going to get a job.'

'*A job!*' At last she had her father's full attention. 'Don't be ridiculous, Alex, of course you're returning to school.'

'No, I'm not. And you can't make me.'

Her father's face was ominously dark. 'And what kind of a job do you propose to get?'

'I don't know. I have "O" levels. I could work in a bank —or a library—or a hospital!'

'A hospital!' Her father latched on to the final assertion. 'And what could you do in a hospital?'

'Lots of things. Train to be a nurse, for one. Or work on the administrative side. It appeals to me.'

Clare rose to her feet, her face cold and angry. 'I think what your daughter really means is that she hopes at some future date to return to the Amazon basin, Professor.'

Alexandra gasped, and Professor Tempest turned to her. 'Is this true, Alex?' he demanded furiously. 'Why on earth should you want to return here?'

'Because she imagines she's in love with Declan!' stated Clare pitilessly. 'She's made nothing but a nuisance of herself to him ever since she arrived!'

Alexandra could only stare speechlessly at them both. She could scarcely believe that Clare would be ruthless enough to tell her father such things.

Professor Tempest's face was grim. 'Good heavens, Alex-

161

andra! Do you hear what Mrs. Forman is accusing you of?' He shook his head. 'Have you nothing to say for yourself?'

Alexandra opened her mouth, but no words would come. She shook her head helplessly, and her father smote a hand to his thigh.

'I can't believe it,' he said harshly, 'I honestly can't believe it! That any daughter of mine should abuse the hospitality of her host by throwing herself at his head. Fortunately I know Declan well enough to realise that he would have no part of it. My God, Alexandra, you deserve a good hiding for this!'

'Excuse, please, *senhor, senhoras*. You would like coffee, *sim*?'

Consuelo was standing in the doorway behind them, her lined face wearing an anxious expression. Professor Tempest's jaw tightened and he shook his head impatiently, but Clare said: 'Thank you, Consuelo. We'll ring if we want anything.'

Consuelo ignored that cold dismissal and looked instead at Alexandra, noticing her pale cheeks, the bruised line around her eyes. 'And you, *senhorita*——?'

'That will do, Consuelo.' Professor Tempest looked at her furiously. 'You have had your instructions from Mrs. Forman. Kindly leave us.'

Consuelo's lips pursed, but she had no choice but to do as he commanded. She went reluctantly through the door and as an afterthought Professor Tempest called: 'Senhor O'Rourke, Consuelo? Where is he?'

'Is out, *senhor*!' returned Consuelo mutinously, and then went away.

'I must speak to Declan,' muttered Alexandra's father bitterly. 'I must apologise——'

'I shouldn't.' That was Clare again, and Alexandra's brows drew together. Surely she wasn't about to defend her? But no, Clare had other axes to grind. 'You'd only

162

embarrass him,' she continued, forcing a persuasive tone. 'He's had enough to contend with without you bringing it all out into the open. Besides, once you're gone . . .'

Professor Tempest pressed his lips together. 'Yes. Yes, perhaps you're right. It would be embarrassing—all round.' He looked again at his daughter, his eyes mirroring his dislike of her at that moment. 'But you and I, Alexandra, we will discuss this again, make no mistake about it. And I don't want to hear any more about you leaving school, is that clear?'

Alexandra turned away, her hands thrust into the hip pockets of her jeans. 'Is that all, Father?' she enquired dully, and sensed his desire to strike her for what he considered downright insolence.

'Yes, that's all for now,' he agreed grimly. 'I suggest you remain in your room for the rest of the day. I'll have your meals sent in to you.'

'Yes, Father.'

Without another word, Alexandra left the room, walking stiffly along the passage to her bedroom. But once there, with the door securely closed, she sank down weakly on to her bed and buried her face in her hands. She had thought things couldn't get worse, but she had been wrong.

Consuelo brought her lunch at about half past one. The old housekeeper came right into the room and closed the door before putting down the tray and saying: 'Is not true, *senhorita*!'

Alexandra looked up wearily. 'What's not true, Consuelo?'

'What the Senhora Forman said, *senhorita*. About herself and Senhor Declan.'

Alexandra made a motion as if pushing something away from her. 'Now, Consuelo, if you've been eavesdropping——'

163

'Eavesdropping, *senhorita*? What is this?'

Alexandra sighed. 'Listening to conversations. Conversations that don't concern you.'

'Is concerning Consuelo!' the housekeeper retorted sharply. 'Consuelo know Senhor Declan since baby.'

'I know that, Consuelo——'

'Senhor Declan never want to marry Senhora Forman. She want to marry him, but Senhor Declan, he leave São Paulo and come to Paradiablo to get away from her.'

Alexandra stared at her incredulously. 'Oh, come on, Consuelo! Why would he do that?'

'Senhor Declan is kind man, *senhorita*. He not want cause trouble—how you say?—hurt feelings!'

'And I suppose you're going to tell me next that Clare married David Forman when she learnt that he was going to work at Paradiablo, too?' Alexandra was sarcastic.

'Is right, *senhorita*. Senhor Forman is dedicated man, too. He want to help Indian.'

Alexandra considered the housekeeper's face for a long uncertain moment. Then she shook her head impatiently. 'Well, it doesn't really matter, does it? One way or the other, she's achieved her objective.'

'*No!*' Consuelo was horrified. 'Is not so. Senhor Declan is—how you say?—friendly, nothing more.'

'How can you be so sure?'

Consuelo drew herself up to her full height. 'Consuelo believe in Senhor Declan. He is not man to take other man's wife.'

Alexandra paced restlessly across the floor. 'I appreciate your loyalty to your employer, Consuelo, but you're wasting your time telling me all this.'

'*Que?*' For once Consuelo was at a loss. 'The *senhorita* is in love with Senhor Declan, *nao*?'

Alexandra's lips tightened. 'Haven't you heard, Consuelo?' she asked bitterly. 'I'm still a schoolgirl! How can I possibly be expected to know my own mind?'

Consuelo plucked unhappily at the strings of her apron. 'The *senhorita* is making fun of Consuelo.'

'No. No, I'm not making fun of you, Consuelo. Of myself perhaps.'

'But—but Consuelo know——'

The housekeeper broke off abruptly, and Alexandra stared at her through narrowed eyes. 'Yes, Consuelo? What do you know?'

Consuelo hunched her shoulders. 'The *senhorita*, she spend night in Senhor Declan's bed.'

Alexandra felt the hot colour flood her cheeks. 'I see.'

Consuelo moved towards the door. 'Consuelo go. You not angry?'

Alexandra shook her head. 'No, I'm not angry, Consuelo. And—and thank you. For your confidence.'

After Consuelo had gone, Alexandra picked at her food. But like the day before she wasn't hungry. Everything seemed to be tumbling about her ears and she wished she could escape from all of them.

About half an hour later her door opened and she looked up in surprise to find Declan entering the room. He closed the door and leant back against it, and she got up from the bed and confronted him tremulously.

'Well? Have you come to demand that I take lunch with you?' she asked unsteadily, 'because I should tell you, my father has forbidden it.'

Declan was unsmiling. 'I know what your father has said.'

'Do you know why?'

'Clare said something about him being angry with you for staying here with me.'

'Oh, did she?' Alexandra chewed her lower lip. She might have known Clare would find some suitable excuse that didn't involve her in any unpleasantness.

165

'Yes. Wasn't it true?'

'Does it matter?' Alexandra turned away. 'Why have you come here? I don't think my father would approve——'

'To hell with your father!' Declan's jaw was taut. 'Alex andra, he said something about you not wanting to go back to school. Is this true?'

Alexandra shrugged indifferently. 'I don't have any say in the matter.'

Declan caught his breath on an expletive. 'Just answer the question.'

'No, I don't want to go back to school. I shall be eighteen in October. Old enough to do what I like. But until then...' She walked slowly towards the window. 'The rain's stopped.'

'Never mind the rain.' Declan was curiously taut himself. 'Alexandra, I have a suggestion to make.'

She glanced round at him. 'Oh, yes?'

'Yes.' He clenched his fists by his sides. 'How would you like to stay with my parents in São Paulo? For a few weeks anyway. It would give your father and his new wife time to get accustomed to one another, and give you a breathing space.'

Alexandra stared at him. 'Stay? With your family? How could I do that?'

'Quite simply. They'd be delighted to have you. And one girl more or less in a houseful of women wouldn't make much difference.'

'But why should you suggest this?' Her heart was palpi tating quite erratically.

'I have no ulterior motive,' he retorted, straightening. 'I simply thought you might enjoy it.'

Alexandra's heart contracted. 'Don't you mean it would let me down more lightly?' she demanded unsteadily. 'A lump of sugar to sweeten the medicine!'

Declan's face hardened. 'Not at all. You obviously can't

166

stay here, and you didn't appear too happy with the new arrangements last night. I was merely trying to make things easier for you.'

'How kind!'

'Oh, it's hopeless talking to you, isn't it? You're so wrapped up in your own self-pity, you don't care who knows it!'

Her lips trembled. 'That's not true!'

'Yes, it is. It never occurred to you that your father might want a woman to share his life, did it? And it doesn't occur to you to welcome her into your family either, does it?'

Alexandra gasped, 'That's not fair!'

'Very little in this life is, is it? Okay, Alexandra, leave it. Go with your father and Juana. Make a martyr of yourself. But don't expect someone to be around to pick up the pieces every time.'

The door slammed behind him and she stood motionless, controlling the racking sobs that rose inside her. Oh, why had she said what she had? Why hadn't she accepted the invitation he so casually offered? At least it would have meant that she could stay in Brazil, be within a thousand or so miles of him! Now she was committed to flying back to England and leaving him to Clare's undoubted attractions.

CHAPTER ELEVEN

DUE, no doubt, to the fact that Alexandra was eating scarcely enough to keep a bird alive and in consequence her resistance to disease was weakened, she developed a severe gastric infection in Rio which confined her to her bed in the hotel for over a week and delayed their departure for England.

Both her father and Juana were most concerned about her and, surprisingly, Alexandra found her stepmother's kindness rather easier to take than her father's helpless anxiety. She got to know Juana quite well during those few days—it was impossible to remain aloof with someone who efficiently changed the sheets when one was sick, and sponged the sweat from one's hot and sticky body—and she began to appreciate exactly why her father had become fond of her. She didn't think it was in her father's nature to really *love* anyone, but his feelings for Juana were as close as he could come.

In her own way, Juana was different from any other woman Alexandra had ever known. She had a shy sensitivity which Alexandra had initially mistaken for confidence, and she was, in fact, a home-loving creature. Her career in bacteriology had been as much determined by the pride in her shown by her parents as through any desire of her own to be independent. And because of this, Alexandra was able to talk to her, about her own feelings towards staying at school and her ultimate ambitions. She didn't discuss Declan with her then, although she suspected at some future date she might. It was distinctly warming after all the trauma of leaving Paradiablo to find she had an unexpected ally.

The effects of the infection itself were rather less reassuring. Alexandra had never carried a lot of weight and now she was positively fragile in appearance, the skin stretched tightly across her cheekbones accentuating the hollows of her cheeks. Her clothes hung upon her, and only in jeans and sweaters did she feel at east. The casual attire concealed the thinness of her legs and arms.

Of course, she was still thinking about Declan, and the knowledge that she was never to see him again squashed any enthusiasm for the delicacies Juana produced for her at mealtimes. Because of her delicate condition, Juana would not allow her to eat anything which she had not personally prepared, and Alexandra felt sure the hotel staff must resent her stepmother's constant invasions of the kitchens.

Still, the sickness and its accompanying unpleasantness ceased, and she was left feeling weak and languid, but no longer nauseated.

The worst part was still to come, of course. Flying home to England presented its own agonies, and she was glad when Juana had the doctor who had attended her in Rio provide her with some sleeping tablets which made the putting of so many miles between herself and Declan easier to bear.

It was good to see Aunt Elizabeth again, although she wasn't so happy about meeting Juana. Her position in her brother's household had never before been threatened and not even Alexandra's father's insistence that everything should remain as it was for the time being could convince her that sooner or later she would not become redundant.

London was sweating in the heat of an unusually dry August, and Professor Tempest immediately suggested that they should all leave for the house he had rented in Cannes.

Alexandra was not keen. Cannes meant young men, friends of business associates of her father's, bikinis, and lots of socialising which right now she was in no state to endure.

Aunt Elizabeth solved the dilemma. 'You go, Arnold,' she said, with a forced smile at Juana. 'You deserve some time alone together. Alexandra and I will stay here. The child's not fit to go travelling again. And besides, she needs good, satisfying British food, not that foreign muck!'

Professor Tempest had protested, of course, but Alexandra could tell he was relieved. As for Juana, she was less willing to abandon her new-found stepdaughter, and the night before they were due to leave she came to Alexandra's room just as she was getting ready for bed. She was sitting before the dressing table. She had been brushing her hair, but the sight of the dark, bruised lines around her eyes had caused her to lean forward to get a closer look and she was touching the corners of her eyes wonderingly when Juana tapped and entered the room.

'I'm not disturbing you, am I?' Juana was always polite.

Alexandra put down the brush and turned on the stool. 'No, of course not, Juana,' she replied, nodding to a basket-weave chair. 'Sit down.'

'Thank you.' Juana seated herself carefully and then looked up. 'Alexandra, I—I wanted to speak to you.'

Alexandra felt a twinge of alarm. 'Yes?'

'Yes.' Juana smoothed her fingers along the arms of the chair. 'It is difficult for me to begin, but ...' She paused. 'First—you do not mind your father and me leaving to-morrow for Cannes, do you?'

Alexandra breathed more easily. 'No, not at all.' She shrugged her slim shoulders. 'I can always join you later, if I want to.'

'Yes. Yes, you could.' Juana smiled, dimples appearing in her plump cheeks. Then the smile disappeared. 'But it was not really to do with this that I have come.'

170

'No?' The tension began again.

'No.' Juana licked her lips. 'Alexandra, your father told me that—that Clare Forman had said that you had been— how did she put it?—making a nuisance of yourself towards Declan O'Rourke?'

Alexandra swung round on her seat. 'I'd really rather not discuss it, Juana.'

'But you must!' Juana moved to the edge of her chair. 'Alexandra, you are making yourself ill! You do not eat— and from the look of your eyes, you do not sleep! This cannot go on.'

Alexandra bent her head. 'Really, Juana, I appreciate what you're trying to do, but——'

'But nothing. Alexandra, this is a dangerous practice. I know. I have seen girls go into declines before.'

'Declines!' Alexandra forced a mockery she was far from feeling. 'Oh, Juana, what an old-fashioned word!'

Juana rose to her feet. 'But its meaning is the same!' she declared impatiently. 'Alexandra, tell me about it. Talk to me! It might help.'

Alexandra heaved a sigh. 'I don't think so, Juana.'

'Why not? Must I assume that Clare was telling the truth and that you are too ashamed to admit it?'

'No!' The protest was out before Alexandra could prevent it. She hunched her shoulders miserably. 'I—I—it wasn't like that.'

'Then what was it like?' probed Juana gently, sitting down once more.

Alexandra hesitated, kicking her bare toes against the teak panelling of her dressing table. 'I—I can't explain.'

'Yes, you can. In confidence, of course.'

Alexandra looked up accusingly. 'You'd tell my father, you know you would.'

'No, I should not. Not if you had asked me not to do so.'

171

Alexandra shook her head. 'I don't know where to begin. You might not believe me.'

Juana smiled. 'I know *you* do not tell lies, Alexandra. I am not so sure about Clare Forman.'

'What do you mean?' Alexandra frowned.

Juana looked doubtful now. 'I'm not sure I should tell you.' Then she sighed. 'Oh, it is simply that Clare has always run after Declan O'Rourke. Why, she even married that poor man, David Forman, just so that she could follow Declan into the mountains.'

Alexandra stared at her incredulously. 'How—how can you know that?'

'I have friends in São Paulo who know the O'Rourkes. Clare created quite a scandal before Declan left for Paradiablo. She embarrassed everyone. Most particularly herself!'

'But she told me that——' Alexandra broke off. 'That is—perhaps I assumed too much.'

Juana eyed her stepdaughter sceptically. 'She told you something about herself and Declan, did she not?' she asked with conviction. 'What was it, Alexandra?'

'I—I probably misunderstood.' Alexandra found it difficult to repeat what the other girl had said.

'Please, Alexandra. You must tell me.'

Alexandra hesitated. 'Oh—oh, well, she said something about Declan being angry because she married David when —when he was away.'

'Oh, what rubbish!' Juana was impatient. 'As far as I can gather, Declan would be most relieved.' She frowned. 'But why would Clare tell you a thing like that anyway?'

Alexandra stroked the silken cord of her dressing gown. 'I—I think she just wanted to make her position clear.'

'But why? If you were such a nuisance to Declan, why should she have to do such a thing?'

172

Alexandra sighed. 'Well, perhaps it was because she saw—well, she saw Declan and me together.'

'What does this mean—together? He was making love to you?' Now Juana sounded astounded.

Alexandra nodded. 'Something like that.'

'*Que!*' Juana sank back in her chair incredulously. 'I do not understand.' She sat up again. 'There was something between you?'

Alexandra drew a trembling breath. 'Not really.' She pressed her palms against her knees. 'He—he thinks of me only as a child.'

'A man does not make love to a child, Alexandra.' Juana was impatient. 'I was afraid of this.'

'Why?'

Juana linked her fingers together. 'Because I do not like to see you getting hurt.'

Alexandra rose to her feet. 'It's a bit late for that, isn't it?'

'I'm afraid it is.' Juana looked down at her hands. 'And when he knew you were leaving? Did Declan say nothing?'

'Oh, yes.' Alexandra's lips curled. 'He said something.'

'What was it?'

'He suggested I might like to go and stay with his family in São Paulo for a few weeks!' Alexandra said bitterly.

'He—invited you to stay with his family?' Juana gasped. 'And what did you say?'

'What do you suppose I said? I didn't want his—charity!'

'Charity? What is this? In that way was this charity?'

Alexandra paced restlessly about the room. 'It was a way to solve his problems, don't you see? It negated any protest I might have made about leaving with you and Daddy.'

'I don't understand.'

Alexandra sighed irritably. 'Don't you? Juana, has it occurred to you that some of what Clare said might have been

173

right, after all? I—I fell in love with him, not the other way about. I wanted him to make love to me. Maybe he was—physically attracted, but if he was it was because—because I encouraged him.'

Her voice broke and Juana rose and went across to her, putting an arm about the painfully thin shoulders, holding her close.

'Oh, Alexandra!' she exclaimed huskily. 'Don't—please don't cry! Try to remember, you are only seventeen—all right, almost eighteen. But you have your whole life ahead of you. Give it a chance. Nothing is ever as black as it seems.'

After Juana had left her Alexandra lay on her bed staring blindly at the ceiling. Talking had released a little of her tension, but it hadn't solved the problem. Nothing could do that!

During the next few weeks, Alexandra made a concerted effort to do as her stepmother had suggested and give life a chance. She dreaded their return from Cannes and their inevitable dismay at her deteriorating appearance. She had even visited a doctor and obtained some tablets to revitalise her appetite, but it was useless. She awoke every morning with the familiar feeling of dread which came from knowing she had to get through another twelve hours before she could swallow another of the capsules which assured her a night's unconsciousness.

Fortunately perhaps, Aunt Liz was too concerned about her own position in the household to pay too much attention to her niece and apart from berating her on occasion for not eating the good food she provided she made little effort to probe the cause.

At the beginning of September they received word that Professor Tempest and his wife would be returning home in a little over a week. The news seemed to galvanise Alex-

174

andra into action. In two weeks her father would expect her to return to school and somehow she had to convince him before that time that she was capable of earning her own living.

But her plans were hampered by a head cold which quickly spread to her chest and put her to bed for several more days. Aunt Liz looked after her competently, but she had none of Juana's gentleness, and seemed to be beginning to find Alexandra's continued ill health more of a nuisance than anything.

'You're due to return to school in a fortnight!' she complained impatiently. 'What on earth are they going to think we've been doing to you? You look like a ghost!'

Alexandra buried her face in the pillows. 'Perhaps I won't be returning to school,' she said in a muffled voice.

'What? Not returning to school? Your father didn't say anything about that to me.'

'I know.' Alexandra pushed the covers away from her feverish body. 'But I don't intend to go back.'

'What nonsense!' Her aunt was uncompromisingly abrupt. 'You just pull yourself together, my girl. You'll be returning to school. What else could you do?'

'I could get a job!'

'A job!' her aunt scoffed. 'What kind of a job could you do?'

'I'd like to train to be a nurse——'

'A nurse!' Her aunt was irritable. 'Nurses need to be reliable, not wan-faced waifs who are blown over by the first puff of wind!'

Alexandra knew her aunt too well to argue. So she let it go, deciding that whatever plans she made she would keep them to herself.

The weekend before her parents were due home. Alexandra was left with only the servants for company. Her aunt had had a letter from an old school friend who now lived in the United States that she was leasing a cottage in Sussex for several weeks, and with it came an invitation for a weekend's visit. To give her aunt her due she had been very doubtful about accepting, even though Alexandra assured her that she was perfectly capable of looking after herself for a couple of days. Secretly, she thought she might have the opportunity to arrange an interview at one of the many London hospitals who always seemed to need student nurses. If she could only accomplish something, have some proof to give her father that she was not as incompetent as he seemed to think...

Aunt Liz left on Friday evening and Alexandra went to bed soon after eight o'clock, swallowing two of her tablets to assure herself of a decent night's sleep. But she seemed scarcely to have closed her eyes before someone was shaking her awake again, someone whose hands were rough and impatient, whose voice was strangely harsh—yet familiar...

She blinked in the light from the lamp that had been lit beside her bed—and then her heart almost stopped beating. She was having hallucinations now, to add to all her other miseries. It could not possibly be Declan who was bending over her, Declan's hands that were shaking her, slapping her, Declan's tongue that was lashing her with words that hitherto she had never heard him use. She closed her eyes to shut out the image.

'For God's sake, Alexandra,' he was saying angrily, 'wake up, can't you? Damn you, what have you done to yourself!'

'Really, sir, I don't know what Miss Tempest would say if she came home and found you in her niece's bedroom!'

Alexandra's eyelids flickered. That was Mrs. Forrest's voice, her father's cook and general factotum. What was Mrs. Forrest doing in her bedroom?

Someone flung back the bedcovers and Mrs. Forrest protested. Cool air flooded over Alexandra's body and she realised belatedly that she was wearing the sheerest of chiffon nightgowns. She tried to gather her wits while strong hands levered her up in the bed and forced her feet to the floor.

'Now that will do!' Mrs. Forrest sounded positively frightened. 'If you don't get out of here this minute, I'll call the police——'

'Go and make some black coffee, Mrs. Forrest, and stop behaving like a panic-stricken mouse! What in God's name has she been taking? Do you know?

Alexandra swayed in a sitting position as Mrs. Forrest said: 'Miss Alexandra's been ill, sir. She takes sleeping tablets—I told you.'

'Okay, okay, go and make that coffee! And stop looking so alarmed. She knows me, I tell you.'

Alexandra thought she heard Mrs. Forrest walk away, but she couldn't have done. None of this was really happening. It was all some horrible nightmare and in a while she would wake up beneath the covers of her bed, not pacing up and down the soft carpet on unsteady legs supported by a grip that was almost cruel in its firmness.

'Alexandra!' Declan's voice was close to her ear now, and she tried to see his face. But he was too close. His face was blurred.

Licking dry lips, she summoned all her strength and said wonderingly: 'Declan?'

'Oh, *God*!' His hold on her brought her suddenly close against the hard length of his body. 'Oh, God, Alexandra!' he groaned, and buried his face in the soft hollow of her neck.

He was trembling, she could feel it, and as the waves of Morpheus began to recede her conscious mind took over. This *was* actually happening, he *was* actually here. And he was holding her in his arms as if he would never let go.

Her lids felt sticky, but at least they no longer clung

together and she looked incredulously round the room. It was just the same as it had been when she climbed into bed—how long ago? She focused on the clock. Ten o'clock! Was that all it was? Had she only been in bed a little less than two hours?

As full recall came to her she became aware of her scanty attire and would have drawn back from him, but he would not le her go. At last he lifted his head and looked down at her, and now she could see the lines of strain which had etched a path from his nose to his mouth. She could see something else, too—the burning anger in his eyes.

'How dare you!' he demanded through clenched teeth. 'How dare you abuse your body by drugging yourself like that!'

Alexandra tried to push him away from her, shocked by the fury in his voice. 'I—I haven't been sleeping well,' she began unevenly.

'Damn you, do you think I have?' His hands gripped her shoulders. 'Why didn't you write to me? Why didn't you tell me——'

'Tell you? Tell you what?' Alexandra quivered.

Declan shook his head grimly, looking down at her, uncaring of her futile attempts to cover herself. 'You're so thin!' he continued, as if she hadn't spoken. 'So thin! Don't you realise how stupid you've been?'

Alexandra tore herself away from him. 'I don't need you to come here and tell me how stupid I am,' she mumbled in a wobbly voice. 'If that's all you've woken me up for, please go away.'

She heard him draw an unsteady breath. 'That's not why I'm here,' he stated bleakly. 'For heaven's sake, where is that woman with the coffee!'

Alexandra pulled on her silk dressing gown. 'Perhaps we'd better go downstairs——'

'Why?' He turned cold eyes on her. 'This is good enough.'

'Mrs. Forrest will tell my aunt——'

'Do you think I care?'

As though in answer to his demand, Mrs. Forrest appeared at that moment carrying a tray. She looked relieved to find that Alexandra was awake and apparently unharmed, but as she put down the tray she said: 'I—I couldn't stop him, miss. He—he practically forced his way in here. I told him you were in bed and didn't want to be disturbed, and he said that nobody went to bed at half past nine!'

Alexandra forced a faint smile. 'That's all right, Mrs. Forrest.'

'He said he knew you, miss.'

'He does,' Alexandra nodded. 'Thank you, Mrs. Forrest. That will be all.'

'Would you like me to stay——'

'No, thank you, Mrs. Forrest.' Declan walked to the door and held it meaningfully and Mrs. Forrest could do no more than leave them, although Alexandra guessed that her aunt would hear of this the minute she got back.

Declan closed the door behind her, leaned against it for a minute, and then walked across to pour the coffee. Alexandra watched him. She had not seen him in a suit before, and the dark blue corded velvet fitted his muscular body closely. His shirt was blue, too, a darker shade, accentuating the darkness of his tan. He had a definitely alien quality in the pink and white luxury of her bedroom.

He brought her a cup of black coffee. 'Drink it!' he commanded brusquely, and she obeyed. He drank his own coffee thoughtfully, and then without asking her permission lit a cheroot. There was nowhere for him to knock his ash, so he opened the door into her bathroom and dropped the ash into the washbasin.

179

When he came back, Alexandra had finished her coffee and was putting down her cup on the tray. He watched her broodingly, the cheroot between his teeth, his hands thrust uncompromisingly into the front pockets of his trousers.

'Well?' he said at last, without taking the cheroot out of his mouth. 'How long have you been like this?'

Alexandra turned away. 'I don't know what you mean.'

'Like this,' he repeated coldly. 'Sick, ill, not eating or sleeping?'

'I—I've had a cold——'

'And the rest?'

'If you must know, I developed a gastric infection before we left South America.' She plucked nervously at the cord of her gown. 'It's taken some time to shake it off.'

'You don't look as though you have shaken it off,' he commented, his eyes raking her mercilessly.

Alexandra shook her head. 'I—I lost some weight, that's all. I—I look better with my clothes on than off. I—I always did.'

'I disagree.' He surveyed her without emotion. 'I have different recollections.'

Alexandra's face burned. 'Yes—well, I'm sorry if you don't approve.'

She was trying to be as composed as he, but her nerves were shattered by his nearness, and she couldn't understand the contempt in his eyes when he looked at her. Tears pricked at the back of her eyes, and she turned away so that he should not see her pitiful weakness. She was unaware until she looked up and saw his reflection in the dressing table mirror that he could see everything.

'Aren't you going to ask me why I'm here, instead of giving in to tears?' he asked harshly.

She swung round, wiping her cheeks with the back of her hand. 'All—all right. Why are you here?'

He tossed the cheroot into the basin in the bathroom and came towards her. 'Juana wrote to me.'

'W-what?' Alexandra was horrified. 'Oh—oh, she shouldn't have done!'

'Why not? Do you know what she said?'

Alexandra shook her head mutely, and he drew an envelope out of his inside pocket, tapping it against his other hand.

'Then I'll tell you. She wrote to thank me for looking after you while you were at Paradiablo.'

'O-oh!'

'That wasn't all.' His jaw tautened and she could see a pulse working away rapidly. 'She also said that you had unfortunately developed a gastric infection in Rio and that in consequence you had been unable to accompany them to Cannes.'

Alexandra pressed a hand to her throat. 'I—I see.' She took a deep breath. 'Was—was that all?'

Declan dropped the letter on to the bed. 'Yes, that was all. Read it! What did you expect?'

Alexandra shook her head. 'I—nothing——'

Declan's face darkened. 'I don't believe you, Alexandra. I think you were afraid she might have told me the truth about you.'

'The truth?' Alexandra felt hopelessly incapable to withstand his anger.

'Yes. But fortunately Juana has some perception. She realised that if, as she believed, I did care about you, the very fact that you had been ill would be sufficient to bring me here to find out.'

Alexandra was shaking so much her legs no longer felt as if they would hold her. 'Declan, I——'

His face contorted with an expression of self-disgust and he reached for her, grasping her cruelly, wrenching her slender body close against the hardness of his.

181

'Crazy, crazy woman!' he groaned, burying his face in her hair. 'Can't you feel what you do to me—what you've always done to me. Only I don't have the right to enjoy it!'

Alexandra trembled violently. 'I—I don't know what you're talking about,' she breathed, pressing her face against the silk of his shirt.

'Yes, you do,' he insisted, holding her face between his hands. 'I'm talking about you—and me—and the fact that I'm too old for you, besides living the kind of life no man should offer to a woman!'

Alexandra's pale cheeks suffused with colour. 'You mean —you mean——'

'I mean I'm in love with you,' he muttered thickly, covering her mouth with his own and silencing her protests effectively.

For a long time there was silence in the room, broken only by the endearments he murmured against her lips, her cheeks, the hollows of her throat. But at last he had to put her away from him, reaching unsteadily for his cheroots.

'All right,' he said, and his tone was grim again. 'You begin to see how it is with me.' He thrust a cheroot between his teeth and lit it with unsteady fingers. 'When I received Juana's letter I was——' He shook his head. 'I knew I had to see you again. To assure myself that you were all right.' He drew her close to him, seemingly unable to keep his hands off her. 'Can you imagine how I felt when I arrived here and found you apparently suffering the effects of a severe sleeping draught?'

'Oh, Declan!' She slid her arms round his waist, herself unable to actually believe that this was really happening. 'You don't know how—how desperate I've been.'

'Don't I?' His eyes were hard. 'Why didn't you accept the invitation to stay with my parents if you felt this way?

182

Why did you have to go scuttling off home like a terrified rabbit!'

'You—don't understand. There—there were reasons—'

'Clare? Yes, I know. Consuelo told me.'

'What did she tell you?'

'About what Clare had said—about the row she had heard between you and your father, ably assisted by Mrs. Forman.'

Alexandra's tongue touched her lips. 'When did she tell you?'

'After you'd gone.' Declan shrugged. 'Oh, don't judge me too harshly, Alexandra. I wanted you, I admit it. I also admit to taking out my frustration on you.'

'That day by the pool——?'

'Yes. That day by the pool.' He compressed his lips derisively. 'I was quite convincing, wasn't I? God knows what would have happened if you hadn't stopped me.' He bent his head. 'You've no idea how much I despised myself.'

'But—why?' She stared at him tremulously.

'Because you were so young—so innocent. And you trusted me. The trouble was, I couldn't trust myself.'

Alexandra touched his cheek. 'I grew up at Paradiablo.'

'I know that. And I blamed myself for that, too.'

'But I wanted to grow up, Declan——'

He sighed. 'It's not that easy, though, is it?' He looked down at her. 'Even now.'

'What do you mean?'

Declan hesitated. 'All right. I accept that I am in some part responsible for this . . .' He touched the dark circles around her eyes.

'You're totally responsible!' she declared unsteadily.

'Perhaps.' He shook his head. 'But that doesn't alter the facts. You're not yet eighteen, and I'm thirty.'

'So what?'

'So—many things. Your father will never agree—you

183

haven't even finished school——'

'I have.' She straightened her shoulders. 'I—I was going to make arrangements to have an interview tomorrow at one of the local hospitals.'

Declan frowned. 'Why?'

'I thought—I might train to be a nurse.' She paused. 'Nurses are always in demand, aren't they?' she asked in a small voice.

'Oh, Alexandra!' He pressed her closely against him, his hands on her hips. 'You really are crazy, do you know that?'

'About you? Yes, I know.'

He took a deep breath. 'All right, all right. I don't think I can hold out much longer.' He looked down at her. 'I suggest you do as I asked in the first place and come and stay with my parents in São Paulo for a while. We'll take it from there.'

Alexandra's eyes clouded. 'But why must I?'

'Because I need you within reaching distance,' he admitted huskily, 'and because it may be one way to convince your father that you are adult enough to know your own mind. We'll wait—I don't know—six months maybe. If you still feel the same in that time——'

'Don't you mean—if you do?' she asked unsteadily.

'Oh, I'll feel the same,' he muttered roughly. 'Do you think I want to do this? Do you think I want to risk you meeting someone else in São Paulo and possibly changing your mind? Enrico, perhaps?'

Alexandra shivered. 'All right. If that's what you want.'

'It's not what I want,' he replied grimly. 'But it's what your father will insist on, and I'm not prepared to alienate my future father-in-law for the sake of a few weeks.'

Alexandra nodded reluctantly. 'You—you will come to see me, won't you?' she asked.

He smiled wryly. 'Try and stop me!'

'And Clare?'

'Oh, Alexandra, when you're my wife, I don't think Clare will find the climate at Paradiablo half so satisfying.' He pushed her gently from him. 'And now I think you ought to get back into bed. You're cold, and I don't want anything else to happen to you.'

Alexandra obediently slid between the sheets. 'Where— where are you staying?' she asked.

He shook his head. 'Nowhere, yet. I only arrived in London a couple of hours ago. I came straight here.'

'Stay here, then.'

'With you?' He shook his head. 'Not tonight, my darling. I really think that would be asking too much!'

Alexandra and Declan were married the following Easter in the church at São Paulo. Declan had so many relatives who wanted to attend, whereas Alexandra only had her father and stepmother and her aunt. Aunt Elizabeth was making the trip en route to the United States where she was going to take a prolonged holiday with the school friend who had visited England the weekend Declan had come to find Alexandra.

Alexandra's dress was of white lace over a satin underskirt, and she carried a sheaf of roses. It was quite an important occasion in the social life of the busy Brazilian city, and guests came from miles around to wish them well. Even Clare managed a sisterly peck on Alexandra's cheek, although she cast an envious glance at her handsome husband, dark and disturbing in his morning clothes.

But so far as Alexandra and Declan were concerned, it was what came after the ceremony that mattered. They flew to Acapulco in Mexico for their honeymoon, and it was there, under the star-studded velvet of the night sky, that she really became his wife, his mate, the one woman in the world he could never deny.

'At last I have the right to share your bed,' he murmured with satisfaction, his mouth seeking the warm curve between her breasts, full and rounded again after her happy weeks staying with his family.

'You always had that right,' she answered sleepily.

Take romance with you on your holiday.

Holiday time is almost here again. So look out for the special Mills & Boon Holiday Reading Pack.* Four new romances by four favourite authors. Attractive, smart, easy to pack and only £3.00.

*Available from 12th June.

Dakota Dreamin' Janet Dailey	**Forbidden Flame** Anne Mather
Devil Lover Carole Mortimer	**Gold to Remember** Mary Wibberley

 Mills & Boon

The rose of romance

Doctor Nurse Romances

and May's
stories of romantic relationships behind the scenes
of modern medical life are:

ACCIDENT WARD
by Clare Lavenham

When Nurse Joanne Marshall's boyfriend is admitted
to *her* ward, she is pleased to be able to nurse him
herself. But the handsome new registrar, Paul Vincent,
appears and her heart is torn in two . . .

HEAVEN IS GENTLE
by Betty Neels

Sister Eliza Proudfoot takes a job at Professor
Christian van Duyl's clinic and falls in love with him.
But then she finds he is already engaged to a placid
Dutch girl . . .

Order your copies today from your local paperback retailer

Masquerade
Historical Romances

Intrigue excitement romance

THE FLAME STONE
by Kate Buchan

Charlotte's return to her childhood home in France was far from happy. In her absence her father had been branded a traitor, and Etienne de Chatigny — the man she loved — had married another girl. But why was the old Count so hated? And why did Etienne behave as though Charlotte had deserted *him?*

A GIFT FOR PAMELA
by Judy Turner

Lord Crispin O'Neill had forgotten to buy a gift for Miss Pamela Courtney, so he felt he had every reason for buying Peri — a most unusual slave girl — to repair his omission. Unfortunately, Miss Courtney loathed Peri on sight, and his lordship had to revise his plans in a hurry!

Look out for these titles in your local paperback shop from 8th May 1981

Mills & Boon
Best Seller Romances

The very best of Mills & Boon Romances
brought back for those of you who missed
them when they were first published.

In June
we bring back the following four
great romantic titles.

PALE DAWN, DARK SUNSET
by Anne Mather

Miranda travelled to Mexico to find out if the child who was
being looked after in a Catholic mission was in fact her niece,
Lucy, who had been given up for dead after an air disaster.
Juan Cueras, who seemed to have adopted the child, was only
too willing to help Miranda. But it was his enigmatical brother
Rafael to whom Miranda felt most drawn . . .

COVE OF PROMISES
by Margaret Rome

With her schooldays in Paris behind her Elise could hardly wait
for her return to Jamaica to be reunited with Jacques, from
whom she had been parted for ten years. Jacques, her childhood
sweetheart, to whom she would soon be married. But Elise was
to find reality very different from the dreams she had cherished,
and the man she thought she knew now seemed an aloof
stranger . . .

COUNTRY OF THE VINE
by Mary Wibberley

Although Charlotte had led a sheltered life she was sure she
could cope with anything that could be considered a problem.
Until, in a French vineyard, she met Jared, the man whose dark
attraction she had never forgotten.

THE VIKING STRANGER
by Violet Winspear

What a fascinating man Erik Norlund was, Jill thought. She
couldn't be sure which facet of him came uppermost — the
smooth American tycoon, or the more rugged characteristics
of his Viking forebears. She got her chance to find out when
Erik offered her a job in his luxury department store in sunny
California.

If you have difficulty in obtaining any of these books through
your local paperback retailer, write to:

Mills & Boon Reader Service
P.O. Box 236, Thornton Road, Croydon, Surrey, CR9 3RU.

The Mills & Boon Rose is the Rose of Romance

Every month there are ten new titles to choose from — ten new stories about people falling in love, people you want to read about, people in exciting, far-away places. Choose Mills & Boon. It's your way of relaxing:

May's titles are:

THE McIVOR AFFAIR *by Margaret Way*
How could Marnie kill this feeling of attraction that was growing between her and the hateful Drew McIvor, whom her stepmother had cheated?

ICE IN HIS VEINS *by Carole Mortimer*
Jason Earle was a cold, unfeeling man. Yet, given the right circumstances, Eden could like him altogether too much!

A HAUNTING COMPULSION *by Anne Mather*
Despite the bitterness Rachel Williams felt about Jaime Shard, she accepted to spend Christmas with his parents. But Jaime would be there too ...

DEVIL'S CAUSEWAY *by Mary Wibberley*
Why did Maria have to complicate the situation by falling in love with Brand Cordell, who was angry and bitter about the whole thing?

AUTUMN IN APRIL *by Essie Summers*
Gaspard MacQueen hoped Rosamond would come and settle in New Zealand, but his grandson Matthieu had *quite* another view of the situation!

THE INTERLOPER *by Robyn Donald*
It was the hard Dane Fowler whom Meredith really feared. All the more so, because of her unwilling love for him ...

BED OF ROSES *by Anne Weale*
Was her husband Drogo Wolfe's involvement with his 'close friend' Fiona turning Annis's bed of roses into a bed of thorns?

BEYOND THE LAGOON *by Marjorie Lewty*
When her deception was discovered Gideon North's opinion of Susan French would hardly be improved. Why did she care so much?

SUMMER OF THE RAVEN *by Sara Craven*
Rowan was stuck with Carne Maitland, the one man she really wanted — and one who was totally out of reach.

ON THE EDGE OF LOVE *by Sheila Strutt*
Dulcie fell in love with the cold Jay Maitland — only to find that his coldness didn't apply to the beautiful Corinne Patterson!

If you have difficulty in obtaining any of these books from your local paperback retailer, write to:

Mills & Boon Reader Service
P.O. Box 236, Thornton Road, Croydon, Surrey, CR9 3RU.

Mills & Boon
Best Seller Romances

The very best of Mills & Boon
brought back for those of you
who missed reading them when they
were first published.
There are three other Best Seller Romances
for you to collect this month.

FORBIDDEN RAPTURE
by Violet Winspear

When Della Neve went on a Mediterranean cruise, she wasn't
looking for a holiday romance. Her future was already bound to
Marsh Graham, the fiancé to whom she owed everything. But on
board ship she encountered Nicholas di Fioro Franquila, who
treated women as playthings. Was Della an exception?

THE BENEDICT MAN
by Mary Wibberley

Lovely surroundings and a kind and considerate employer —
Beth was delighted at the prospect of her new job in Derbyshire.
But when she arrived at Benedict House she discovered that it
was not the sympathetic Mrs. Thornburn who required her
services as a secretary, but her arrogant and completely unreason-
able nephew. Could Beth put up with his insufferable attitude
towards her?

TILL THE END OF TIME
by Lilian Peake

As far as Marisa was concerned Dirk was no longer part of her
life. So it came as a great shock to her when he returned, even
more dictatorial and exasperating than she remembered him,
to disrupt her calm again. Of course, it wasn't as if he meant
anything to her now. Yet why did she find herself wondering
about his relationship with the glamorous Luella?

If you have difficulty in obtaining any of these books through
your local paperback retailer, write to:

Mills & Boon Reader Service
P.O. Box 236, Thornton Road, Croydon, Surrey, CR9 3RU.